on o

DELOUME ROAD

DELOUME ROAD

MATTHEW HOOTON

JONATHAN CAPE
LONDON

Published by Jonathan Cape 2010

2 4 6 8 10 9 7 5 3 1

Copyright © Matthew Hooton

Matthew Hooton has asserted his right under the Copyright, Designs
and Patents Act 1988 to be identified as the author of this work

First published in Great Britain in 2010 by
Jonathan Cape
Random House, 20 Vauxhall Bridge Road,
London SW1V 2SA

www.rbooks.co.uk

Addresses for companies within The Random House Group Limited can be found at:
www.randomhouse.co.uk/offices.htm

The Random House Group Limited Reg. No. 954009

A CIP catalogue record for this book
is available from the British Library

ISBN 9780224087650

The Random House Group Limited supports The Forest Stewardship
Council (FSC), the leading international forest certification organisation. All our
titles that are printed on Greenpeace approved FSC certified paper carry the FSC logo.
Our paper procurement policy can be found at:
www.rbooks.co.uk/environment

Mixed Sources
Product group from well-managed
forests and other controlled sources
www.fsc.org Cert no. TT-COC-2139
© 1996 Forest Stewardship Council
FSC

Printed and bound in Great Britain by
CPI Mackays, Chatham, ME5 8TD

For Dad, Mom and Joel

Back on the road, I thought, How must it be
now, and now, us disappearing? And now, us
gone? And now, the road empty?

— RAY BRADBURY,
"The Kilimanjaro Device"

The Road

A berry-stained ice cream pail with a shoelace for a handle sits in the wheat grass beside Deloume Road. The boy next to it has white-blond hair and a sun-freckled nose. He lets his hand, full of blackberries, hover over the pail. The child hesitates, his cobalt eyes studying each berry in case one is too ripe for the pail, then tips his hand.

A mangy dog with patches of brown and black fur pauses at the sound of the berries hitting the plastic and trots over to sniff the bucket before continuing down the road, one ear flopping with each step, past potholes, crabapple trees and a neglected stop sign that rusts and curls on its wooden pole.

Just over the Malahat pass with the old Bamberton cement works behind you on Highway 1 heading north on Vancouver Island, take a left onto Shawnigan Mill Bay Road. Pass dairy farms, orchards and a cidery, each isolated along the road, as if dropped into massive and seemingly timeless clearings from the sky—no hint that this land was painstakingly carved out of forest by hand, horse and dynamite nearly a century ago. There aren't any towns here, and few businesses to speak of, only roads sparsely littered with houses and the occasional farm shop, all of it a wilderness suburb of the small town of Mill Bay. Five miles or so of this, then on your left Deloume Road begins at the top of a hill. There is no need for a No Through Road sign because there isn't anywhere to pass through to—Deloume Road far enough from coastline and so deep in wilderness that it feels like it inhabits its own continent at times, a world removed from even the smell of salty air, the forest on the edge of the rain shadow, dryer and warmer in summer than the dark temperate rainforest farther north, but still dense, tall and green, full of mossy conifers and arbutus.

Deloume Road is covered with loose gravel and the sunken patch at the bottom of that first steep hill is impossible to drive over without scratching a car's exhaust pipe. The children of Deloume ride bikes down this hill, dust and gravel flying up behind. At the bottom they pull back on handlebars and jump off the divot, then hit back-pedal brakes and skid sideways. Men drive past this spectacle with too much care, as though shocked by the memories evoked. They consider the scratched exhaust pipes beneath their seats, and make unspoken measurements of the road and of their cars, trying to suppress the panic of excitement they feel when the bike tires lift off, and the profound sorrow of middle age that creeps into the passenger seats beside them when the dust settles and they see the long snaking skid marks in the gravel.

The only driveway off this steep hill leads to a derelict house, where artists and leftover hippies practise landscape painting and cultivate marijuana, and where cows have become famous in portraits without knowing it. This house isn't part of the neighbourhood proper, and it stands like a gatehouse to the road ahead, paint peeling from its wooden siding.

The first half mile of road from the bottom of the hill is flanked by farmland on each side: on the right, cows graze beyond electric-lined wooden fencing that starts thirty feet from the road, and on the left, rotten wooden poles and barbed wire run right alongside the gravel, and the sweetness of pig manure hangs heavy in the air. On the pig farm the boards of an enormous roofed trough have turned grey with the weather, and the land around it is laid waste by hundreds of sows and their offspring. Crows sit on the telephone lines along Deloume here, drawn to the mounds at the back of the farm where diseased pigs are buried. When the farmer is out of sight, they will flock to the earth and scratch with their beaks and talons, uncovering a limb or a hip, then tear at the hide and eat whatever flesh they can find, keeping watch all the while. If a child stops beside the fence to pick up a stone, the crows will scatter.

Blades of grass grow waist-high along both sides of Deloume, and tangles of blackberry bushes and crabapple trees border the dairy farm in patches, filling in the space between the road and fence, cutting the cows off from view in places. Children stop here in August, laying their bikes in the grass on the roadside and wandering deep into the mess of thorns and branches, eating berries as they go, until it appears from the road that they are impossibly far in and must have sprung up from the fertile ground. They pick sour apples and bite into them, squinting and chewing their bottom lips as they wait for the sourness to pass, the bitterness sharper because of the blackberries they've eaten. The smell of overripe berries and the buzzing of fat insects surrounds them. That night the children will have stomach aches but won't complain in case their mothers see their stained fingers or thorn-scratched arms and know.

The farmland past, the road travels through maples that reach across and touch leaves, forming a shady tunnel, and a narrow river flows beneath that, dividing the farmland from the rest of the neighbourhood. Children spend their summer holidays beside the pool at the end of the stacked metal pipes that allow the river passage under Deloume, trying to catch small trout with fishing rods made from red cedar branches and hooks stolen from tackle kits and fastened to shoelaces with a few inches of real fishing line. When the river slows to a trickle in August, the children will explore it as far as they can walk and still won't find its source before dinner. The river smells of rust and the river is endless.

Just beyond the river a stop sign stands without reason, placed there by the government and ignored by drivers. It faces the other side of the road, and nearly every child that walks past throws a rock, aiming for the open space between the T and the P, where bullets have cut through the metal.

Up a small hill from this valley of farmland and riverbed is the heart of the road, where the gravel has been steamrolled with tar and is less dusty. Along this final half mile of Deloume long driveways appear every few hundred feet on each side, and some of the homes' TV antennas are visible from the road, the haphazard metal ladders reaching towards the heavens in hopes of picking up the CBC or maybe a channel from Bellingham or Seattle. In winter, chimneys give off smoke signals, messages from house to house reminding families that they are not alone in the wilderness, that the forest separating them isn't infinite. The signs at the ends of driveways are numbered out of order and can't be separated from family names: 1204, 1217, 1212; Ford, Henry, Choi. Twelve driveways in all.

Scotch broom spreads along the sides of the road and up the edges of driveways, choking saplings and flowering in butterfly-blossom yellow each spring. And along the road and between houses are alder and cedar too, maple, pine, fir and hemlock. Acres of seemingly impenetrable Oregon grape and salal, huckleberry, salmonberry and blackberry. There are stinging nettles, wild strawberries and honeysuckle.

And now the road continues its slow winding climb past the final few driveways, until Deloume ends in a silver metal gate that is the private entrance to an overrun hobby farm, where cows, sheep, goats and chickens live, and where the owners come and go and feed the animals too much and don't harvest their fields.

This is the end of the road, but if you turn around, it's the beginning.

It's easiest if you sit with me on the road. If you watch the breeze weave through the tops of the Scotch broom. If you ignore the dusty gravel and tar and instead focus on the tangle of wild blackberry vines at your feet. There's only one berry on the vine and it's covered with dust from the occasional passing car. In the distance a woodpecker rattles off Morse code.

When I sit down the tall grass bends beneath me and I wipe sweat from my forehead. You sit beside me, your feet in the ditch. Heat waves rise from the road into green branches and then disappear into blue sky. Insects hum unseen. A car backfires as its engine turns over somewhere up the road. Dogs bark, first at the noise and then at each other. Finally the car rolls into view heading towards the farms, gaining speed as it passes us on its way out. I squint to see the licence plate, try to memorize it before it's out of sight.

"I didn't think you'd still be here," I say.

A dandelion top blows past and you reach out. It drifts to within an inch of your palm and then catches a current and floats over your small hand.

I tell you I want to explain. And show you the place as I saw it then. Before it happened.

A yellow flower from the Scotch broom falls at my feet. The connector box on the telephone pole gives off an electric whine. The dogs stop barking. A grasshopper's wings unsheathe as it springs into the air beside me and takes flight.

My eyes wander along the bottom of the ditch to a snake-skin lying in the dry grass beside us, almost invisible beneath the roots and tangle of blackberry vines. I watch as the sun dries and curls the lampshade hide. Wood ants pass over it in a thin black and red line.

I can feel your eyes on my skin.

The woodpecker hammers against a different tree. The wood is harder and the sound sharp. The line of ants has started carrying away tiny pieces of the snake's castoff. I wonder out loud how long it will take them to haul the whole thing.

You look at me and stand up.

I follow suit, brushing dust from my legs and backside and stepping onto the road. The red-crested woodpecker swoops over us.

"I never forgot the smells. Like dust, and then rain on a dusty road. And sounds. Like dry leaves under bare feet and moth wings in your ear at night. And then there's the trees and bushes."

My words hang on the breeze. You stand looking down the road towards the river.

"That one's an arbutus," I say quickly, pointing. "Its bark peels like skin."

I pick a long stem of wild grass as you start walking. Heat waves rise and waver around your ankles and then shimmer higher, your outline blurring into moving colours, fading like a trick of the light, threatening to leave me alone on the road.

MATTHEW

He sat on the ground beside the driveway, hidden by alder saplings, clutching a bundle of uprooted bracken ferns, their shafts three feet long and mature. He'd peeled off their leaves and the root ends were pointed like arrowheads and still brown from the earth.

He sat still, cross-legged, breathing slowly to steady himself and make as little noise as possible. The ground smelled like roots and fiddleheads, and his green T-shirt and brown denim shorts blended into the underbrush. Beneath his eyes finger-width lines of mud dried into war paint, pulling his skin taut.

I am Hawkeye.

A dog barked in the Fords' lot. Late summer bees wafted overhead, heavy with pollen, humming on and off in perfect meter, as if their wings were failing propellers stopping and starting in mid-air.

The crunch of tires on gravel, slow, then gaining momentum. His hands began to sweat as he chose a spear for the first strike. It had to be perfect. As the bike passed, he leapt to his feet and shouted a war cry, throwing the first spear through the spokes of his brother's rear wheel, where the weapon folded, its sinews twisting and breaking and winding around the bike chain.

The bike stopped and Andy leapt off as it fell, whimpering and hopping sideways. Matthew threw a second spear at his brother, who turned so the point glanced off his shoulder. Andy looked down at his bike, as if trying to decide whether or not to leave behind a wounded friend, then ran back up the driveway towards the house. Matthew launched two more spears after him, one missing completely, the other striking his brother on the back of his calf, causing him to stumble and then run faster.

He didn't follow. Instead, he stood over the bike and waited for Andy's loping run to carry him out of sight.

Retarded.

The word came to him but he shrugged off the guilt. He heard the door of the house slam shut as he dragged the bike into the ferns and low alders, covering it with leaves and branches before hiding himself again.

Cross-legged, breathing fast, listening: bee, woodpecker, dog, car muffler on Deloume. His breathing slowed and he recalled Andy's shocked face, blue eyes wide, blond hair matted and sweaty. And then those same old questions: Why had Andy been born that way? Why hadn't *he*? He pushed them back, leaning against the partially covered bike in the underbrush beside him. Fern spears didn't hurt much but they worked fine for an ambush.

He smiled and his top lip stuck to his teeth.

He'll be back.

ANDY

He stood inside holding the door handle. Chest burning. Dirty pants. Dirty shirt. Spears. His hands trembled.

Be careful.

He locked the door. Sweat dripped off his chin and onto his grey Velcro running shoes.

Fast.

He laughed.

"Fast shoes," he said.

He didn't turn on the hall light or take off his shoes. He imagined crawling into a kitchen cupboard upstairs, closing the door, breathing the dark air.

Bike.

He looked down at his feet again. Road Runner. Flash. Mighty Atom. He turned the handle of the door. The push lock popped, the metal spring vibrating within the brass.

Be careful. Bike.

He stepped outside, the dirt and gravel loud beneath his feet.

"Fast shoes," he said, and started running down the driveway. The green on each side of him blurred, his legs moving so fast he couldn't feel his feet. As he came to the place in the driveway where he'd been ambushed, something clicked inside his head, came unlocked, and he remembered why he was there. He stopped suddenly and looked around. His bike was gone.

"Bike," he said, staring at the skid marks where it had hit the ground.

"Pssst," came a sound from the bushes beside the driveway.

He faced the sound and squinted into the green. "Be careful," he said.

"Pssst. Come here."

He hesitated, then took a step. "No hitting," he said. "Bike?"

Silence. Quiet green. He peered into the undergrowth, fingering the earth stain on his shoulder. Ferns moved.

He pushed his way through them and stumbled over Matthew sitting cross-legged holding a fistful of spears, war paint beneath his eyes. Andy sat and crossed his legs too, pulling his runners beneath him. He saw the metal frame of his bike covered in leaves, but kept quiet. The ground smelled like old shoes.

His brother held the point of a spear up to his face and he closed his eyes. The earthy tip touched each cheek. Then his brother's finger beneath each of his eyes, spreading the dirt into war paint. He itched to touch it, to cover his entire face with it, but he sat on his hands.

Don't touch. Be quiet.

Next his brother uprooted two more ferns, stripped off the leaves and handed them to him. He swallowed as he took the spears. His brother raised a finger to his lips and he nodded.

Be quiet.

He imitated Matthew's breathing. Slow. Matthew looked straight ahead and he did the same, trying to be patient, trying not to check what his brother was doing.

They were waiting for something. Up and down in his stomach. Butterflies. He looked down at the ferns in his hands, one in the right, one in the left.

Two. Two.

Bike tires crunched on gravel as someone turned off Deloume and began pedalling up their driveway towards them.

JOSH

He lay staring at the overhanging branches and leaves. The gravel from the driveway dug into his back and he fidgeted until the pain shifted. Broken ferns lay scattered and bent around him.

He watched a moth drift and flutter over him, white on green, sunlight through its wings. He lifted his head and looked around. His bike was gone and Matthew and Andy were out of sight.

He wondered if they were still watching. Around him short skids and divots marked where he'd fallen off his bike in a shower of spears and war cries.

They'd even had war paint this time.

He'd dropped and played dead because it was easy. If he'd run they might've chased him, and he'd just eaten breakfast. Andy's ferns had all missed, but one of Matthew's had hit his chest. He brushed the dirt off the front of his shirt without sitting up.

Some best friend. He was bigger and stronger than Matthew. He could have fought back, but he didn't want to. Not against Matthew. Or Andy. He wondered if he'd have to walk home without his bike later. He would if he had to, but he was pretty sure they'd give it back soon. Matthew needed him. After all, his friend was awfully skinny.

A grasshopper leapt and opened its wings beside him, disappearing into a patch of nettles.

Maybe later they could all ride over to the deli and see if the butcher would give them some pepperoni.

"Pssst," came a sound from the ferns beside him.

August, 1899

He'd have called it Bald Mountain if anyone had asked. Dry
shrubs poked from cracks in the sun-bleached rocks above
the ring of the treeline, and only the occasional arbutus clung
to a crevice and dug its roots into the wind-whipped terrain
of the round summit.

The forest a thousand feet below was thick and green.
So hard to imagine the density of it from above—branches
draped with beard lichen, walls of salal to hack through and
moss-covered windfalls with ferns growing out in all directions.
He could just make out the tall, lightning-struck Douglas fir,
a giant among giants, a signpost marking his land. The
promised land.

Eagle's hook-beaked cry of salvation above, and wind
through the August-dry leaves of the arbutus before him. He
imagined himself hanging from a thick, peeling branch, his
body swaying in the breeze, maybe for days, his sun-dried
skin turned brown and leathery, pockmarked from the crows
and turkey vultures that would descend on him.

He tied the rope to the thickest branch and wrapped it
into a noose. He had an impulse to carve an epitaph into the
tree. *Gerard Deloume. Died 1899.* But then the tree's bark would
peel and his name would disappear.

AL HENRY

He sat outside on his deck in the bright morning light. Deloume Road was barely visible through the trees, and in the distance he could just make out the crown of Mount Baldy. He scanned the sky out of habit for any sign of a plane.

His son was flying supplies and medicine up north again. Somewhere along the Alaskan border. Nothing up there but elk, bear and trees. Nothing but green, at least the parts they hadn't logged yet. So his son told him.

And then he did see a plane, just a little thing with floats. Probably a modified DHC-2 Beaver, but it was hard to tell from so far off. Sounded about right though. The noise continued for a moment, until other noises from his memory took over: MiGs overhead, mortar fire and the glottal tangle of shouted Korean.

"Al?" Beth's voice snapped him out of it. "You still out here?" Her head popped out the door and she smiled at him, her short grey hair sticking to her forehead in the heat. "I made us some breakfast, come inside."

He smiled back and stood up. It was happening more often now. And Korea forty years behind him. Beth held the door open and he left the porch, wondering just what in the hell was the matter with him, and whether or not it all had something to do with Irene Choi up the road.

IRENE

She sat on a cushion staring at her feet, her ankles swollen to what seemed like twice their normal size. Like her friend Yu-jin's had been, eight months pregnant and sitting cross-legged on the floor of her massive apartment in Seoul. Only nine months married. And it had been arranged for her. Her father was a politician, and he'd wanted a good match, not a love marriage that might make the family look bad.

"He did it for me too," Yu-jin had said.

"No," Irene had replied. "He did it for status."

"Don't you see that both can happen at the same time?"

Yu-jin had a point. She was taken care of for life. All she had to do was give birth and raise a few children. No small task, but then, no job, no worries about money or respect. Irene thought of the view from Yu-jin's apartment, out across the city, over the Han River, all the way to the granite mountains, high and jagged, their tops hazy through the pollution.

Her friend had raised her brown tattooed eyebrows. "I'm not telling you what to do, but if you marry a foreigner you know what people will say."

She flexed her back and caught herself yawning yet again. Perhaps her mother was right. Perhaps she should return to Korea as soon as the child was born. But she shied away from picking up the phone, instead opening the address book that sat on the coffee table beside her and reading through names in Korean and English, each with a number and address beside it. She laid it back down on the coffee table. The worn oak surface was covered with stains, rings and scratches. *Scars,* she mouthed in English. And then she thought in Korean: *No, hieroglyphics of domesticity.*

She wrote her Korean name on the table with her finger in Hangul. Then *Irene* in English. She didn't even know what it meant. And it was difficult to pronounce properly. *Sue Hwa* meant "water flower," and she tried to think of the English translation. Something like a lily, that needed lots of water. Why hadn't she just asked to be called Lily? Not that it was any easier to say.

The baby kicked. It wouldn't be long now. She felt a twinge of panic surface through layers of fatigue. Beth would help her through it. She was a nurse and she'd seen hundreds of births. But then what?

The room was too warm and she stood and pulled open the sliding glass door. A breeze rustled through the draped cedar boughs as she stepped out onto the patio, whispers in Korean, rumours of her running off to Canada. The wind was too gentle to move the chimes above the door, but the skin on her arms goosebumped. She shivered and then relaxed, watching the play of sunlight through leaves on her toes. She heard the faint whine of the flying insects that lived in the massive stump beside her driveway, the one with the bush growing out of the top. She'd picked perfectly round red berries from it earlier that summer, each one like a tiny paper new year's lantern, but it had seemed wrong without Joseph, without the husband who'd taught her the words: *huckleberry, cedar, ant.*

When he had smiled, lines had formed beneath his eyes and a dimple had appeared on his left cheek. His skin had always been tanned, and he'd had thick, dark brown hair. No grey.

When they were first married, she'd told him she loved how he was Korean and not Korean.

"Korean Canadian," he'd corrected.

She'd usually liked it when he helped her with English. Not that time. She'd been upset, told him that it was like living with a grammar teacher, reminded him that she never corrected his Korean, no matter how bad it sounded.

Shame came over her like humidity. How could she still hold a grudge? And did she even remember exactly what he looked like? What parts of him had she forgotten? She scanned his face and body in her mind as if going over a checklist. Each scar, one through his right eyebrow, the moles on his back, how many were there? Was this how it was? Remembering and forgetting over and over? She was starting to feel guilty when she didn't feel sad. The ache was getting duller, and like bones' memory to heal, something inside her was knitting itself back together without her willing it to happen. She sighed and heard herself. In Hangul there was a word for it. The unravelling and softening of memory and pain. But she couldn't think of it, her Korean shrinking as her belly grew.

As she took a deep breath and her stomach pushed out, a squirrel ran up one of the cedars, its feet moving in a blur. It stopped to look at her, then wound around the tree, up and in and out of branches, around the trunk out of sight. Irene laughed, covering her mouth with her hand. She scolded herself and let her hand drop to her side. Joseph had hated that habit.

But it wasn't really a habit. It was a custom. Polite.

Her feet and back ached when she stood in one spot for too long. She felt short of breath, as though she'd been running, and heartburn was climbing its way up from her stomach.

"I never felt slower," she said to the squirrel in Korean.

She eased herself into a white lawn chair, listening for the plastic to strain and crack as she put her full weight on it. The baby hiccuped and she laughed. Everything around her moved. The breeze carried dandelion tops, and birds and clouds passed overhead. She stared up into the sky and felt it begin to turn, as though she weren't anchored to the ground. She gripped the armrests of the plastic chair and took another deep breath, waiting for the feeling of vertigo to pass.

I'm feeling the earth spin, Joseph. Where are you? You are in it now, and you are spinning. Everything moves.

THE BUTCHER

He looked down at the boy and raised an eyebrow. Secretly he loved how shy the children were, and he played off this, stepping around the counter in his bloodstained white apron and crossing his arms in front of his chest.

"What do you want?" he asked, allowing his accent to spill thick from his tongue, and knowing full well the boy was there to beg for pepperoni sticks. Most of the kids in the neighbourhood came by once a week or so. In the Ukraine a child wouldn't have dared ask for a handout, but things were different here.

Matthew stumbled forward, pushed slightly from behind, and the butcher saw the shadow of another child, maybe two, stretching through the door frame. Josh and Andy no doubt.

"How, um, sorry, uh, howmuchpepperonicanwegetforthis?" asked Matthew, dropping three dimes and three pennies onto the spotless counter.

The money rattled on the metal surface and the butcher tried to hide his surprise. He hadn't counted on them having money.

"Let me see," he said, unwrapping two eight-inch sticks from leathery white paper and placing them on the scale. He'd set them aside the day before for this very moment. "Don't you have a brother?" he asked Matthew, this time catching his accent slightly and using his teeth to pronounce the words as clearly as he could. "So high?" He held his hand level with Matthew's shoulder. Matthew nodded and the butcher took out another five-inch piece of pepperoni and pretended to weigh it carefully. "Here," he said, rewrapping the sticks of spiced meat and handing them to Matthew. "But the small piece is for your little brother, ya?" He cringed as the "ya" slipped out.

Matthew nodded, turned and started to run out the door after his friend and brother, then stopped. "Thanks," he said.

The butcher waved the child away. "You paid for it." His hair stuck to his forehead and he felt beads of sweat run down the lines of his face. "Don't forget about your brother, okay?"

The boy nodded again and ran outside.

He sighed and stepped back from the counter. Thirty-odd cents. How long would it be before he saw another customer? Not that it really mattered though. The man who owned the deli and the pig farm made his money selling pigs, not ham. The deli was just something for the locals. Although he couldn't help but wonder how long the owner would keep it open if more people didn't come. And what would that mean for him? The glass case beneath the counter was filled with cuts of pork and he breathed in the spiced and smoked air. He wiped sweat off his forehead with his shirt sleeve. It was too hot to be inside. He turned and walked out the back door of the store.

Sunlight filtered through the overhanging branches of a tree, beyond which stood a small cottage that backed onto the farm, a ten-acre plot that had dried and cracked into a desert over the past two months. He'd never own the land, but he took a small salary for his work and the owners let him live in the cottage. Pigs shuffled in their roofed feeding stalls, their squeals echoing down Deloume Road, which bordered one side of the farm.

He walked to the tall tree and leaned against its grey bark. A breeze shuffled the leaves overhead. The far side of the farm was slightly blurry, but he began counting the pigs in the field out of habit, stopping at thirty-three as crows flapped onto the telephone wires along Deloume.

"Crows," he whispered to himself, smiling. His vocabulary was improving even if his eyesight wasn't. The Dutchman who used to work in the storefront had never learned more than a few sentences. But he was different. Just a little more practice and he'd be able to tell stories and really talk to the customers who drove in from Mill Bay. The way it should be. He rubbed his eyes and they started to water instantly. He'd forgotten to wash the pepperoni spices from his hands. Through the tears that formed as he squinted across the farm, he envisioned his own son running towards him. He opened his mouth to warn him about the barbed wire but caught himself.

He wiped his eyes on his sleeve and glanced at his watch, a wedding gift from Maria's parents. It was too late to make a trip to the bank. He'd been sending money home to his wife and son in the Ukraine for months. Petr would be getting taller, especially since they had money for fresh milk and good cuts of meat now. His boy had always been too thin, and his deep brown eyes appeared sunken. And Maria. A blur of curly brown hair and white teeth. Finally she would have books to read. He tried to blink the remaining spices from his eyes but couldn't.

He'd come here ahead of them to get things started. There were plenty of people from the Ukraine in Canada but none close enough to see often. He'd imagined Canada as a land of opportunity, a place where everything would be easy. It had been naive and a cliché of course, but somehow the idea had lingered. And he had to admit things were much better than they were at home, even with the Wall down in Berlin and the Soviets loosing their grip. Of course he probably should have tried harder to find work in a city, where there were more jobs, but where in a city would he find work that provided him with such cheap accommodation?

His first two months in Canada had been a slow crawl westward. Cousin to cousin. Friends of friends. Nighttime janitorial work, *under the table*, as they said. Buses from Toronto to Winnipeg to Calgary to Vancouver. And then a chance meeting with a Dutchman on holiday whom he'd accidentally greeted in Ukrainian. After a long talk in broken English the man had offered to introduce him to the owner of a pig farm on the island. Said he'd wanted to move on so he could live in a city for a while. And the farm owner had been happy enough to hire an experienced butcher. *Old world charm*, he'd said. And here he was.

It worried him that his family had only sent one letter so far. But he'd left to support them, to send them money so they could come to him, not spend money on stamps. Maria was better off putting every cent into language school for their son. When they arrived it would help if Petr knew a little English at least.

As he turned back towards the shop his heartbeat quickened. If he worked long and hard enough, one day a young man would approach him and greet him in perfect English. And he'd respond in English. He imagined his son's smile. Who would be most proud of whom? They wouldn't need letters then. It was why he practised.

MILES FORD

He grabbed a cold chicken leg from the fridge and sneaked out of his parents' trailer into the junkyard, yawning as he sat down on one of the stripped tires on the edge of the driveway.

Used tires, furniture and skeletal car frames littered the yard, along with television sets without screens, radios by the dozen and miles of tangled electrical wire. He'd heard what people said about the place. They called it the ashtray of the neighbourhood. Said most of the stuff was stolen. He didn't know anything about that though.

He had an older brother and sister but he didn't see them much. His brother worked at the mill and his sister lived with her boyfriend an hour north in Nanaimo. Miles yawned again and looked at the Doberman, its black leather collar chained to a rusting green refrigerator halfway up their potholed driveway.

The night before he'd been woken from his sleep several times by trucks dropping off or picking up pieces of metal or wire or car parts. He couldn't see how his dad made much money from it, but at least a couple of mornings a week the yard was transformed by new piles of uneven lumber or wobbly stacks of hubcaps.

His father had hit him with a rusting car antenna yesterday, and as he rubbed the welts on his arms and shoulders he wondered whether he might go to school that coming fall, even just to get away from home. Although it hadn't gone well last time. Kids telling him he stunk, asking him what dump he found his clothes in.

He finished eating and rinsed off his hands and face with a garden hose. He tightrope-walked between dry potholes past the dog to the end of the driveway. A car's side mirror lay on the ground facing up. He leaned over it and smiled into the cracked glass. His reflection was far away and distorted. Maybe the glass was bent. Was that why his hair was the wrong shade of brown and his teeth were crooked? He ran his tongue over his top teeth. They felt smooth. Why didn't they feel like they looked?

He paused at the end of the driveway where it joined Deloume. Matthew and Josh pedalled past him on their bikes, ignoring him as they made their way along the road. Then came Andy, lagging behind as usual, stretching to move the pedals, one leg circling unevenly, as if one side of the bike were too big. Andy's lopsided pace quickened as the two older boys pulled farther ahead.

Matthew and Josh stopped. They were eating pepperoni sticks from the butcher.

"Hurry up!" Matthew shouted.

Andy's legs moved faster until he reached the two older boys and paused, leaning over the handlebars to catch his breath. Matthew shook his head and bent down to tie Andy's shoelace, which dangled, threatening to wrap itself around a pedal. Miles clenched his teeth, waiting for the two older boys to do something mean. But when Matthew had finished tying the shoelace he just handed Andy some of the pepperoni, and the three of them sat there eating it.

The sound of a car engine across the street at the Henrys' place started, stopped, and started again. The car rolled down the driveway and out onto the road, Mrs. Henry at the wheel, veering to miss a pothole and then the boys on their bikes before disappearing. Deloume Road was quiet in the wake of the motor. Then the Doberman's bark shook the air and Miles shifted his feet on the dry ground. The gravel crunched. All of the things that happened here happened without him. He was invisible. His chest was tight and he coughed. He imagined his lungs made of metal, like submarines, and he sucked in air, holding his breath deep within his pressure-dented lungs.

AVRIL

She stood on the front porch and watched her boys run— Matthew down the curved driveway out of sight, and Andy falling behind, then stopping and returning to the garage where they'd parked their bikes a moment earlier. Matthew looked for all the world like he'd been put together for a parenting magazine. Rarely out of breath or breaking a sweat, coordinated just like his father. His body still childlike but streamlined somehow, a swimmer's build. Then there was Andy: all thumbs and no rhythm, short and skinny for his age. Still, he didn't let it stop him from chasing after his brother. Neither she nor David had blond hair, so Andy's had been a shock right from the start. Still was. Nearly white after a summer outside. And those bright blue eyes. God, they just took her breath away sometimes.

They'd be back in school in a few weeks. Labour Day had a way of sneaking up. At the end of June it seemed so distant, and then, just when having the boys home became routine, they were gone again. Matthew in grade five this year and Andy three back. Sort of. Special ed classes.

She could hear Andy rummaging around in the garage, looking for who knew what. How many times had she asked David to help her clean it out? She'd have to call Bob Ford over from next door and see if he could use any of their old junk.

Maybe he'd even buy some of it. She glanced at the forest separating their properties. The Fords' lot had been quiet all day for a change. It was rare that she didn't hear a motor or somebody banging away on something. Even music sometimes. Thank God she couldn't see the place.

She'd asked Matthew why he and Josh never played with Miles Ford and her son had just shrugged. Told her he didn't know. That the boy was weird. It bothered her that Miles might be lonely in such a small neighbourhood, but then the boys didn't play with Katie or Elaine up the street either, and she didn't complain about that. Matthew and Josh didn't leave much room for anyone else. Even Andy got left out most of the time.

Ten years ago she'd been worried about moving to the island. Let alone out to Deloume. The trees so dense and claustrophobic along their strip of road. But her mother had convinced her in the end. Told her the island was too good an opportunity to pass on, that Matthew would benefit growing up there, that the Prairies were changing, and maybe not for the best. Unless she wanted Matthew to work the oil fields. An exaggeration, but she'd been right about the island being a good place for kids. And her parents had come out from Calgary every year for Christmas, and at least once more each summer. Until last year. Her mom's first stroke had come in May. Then a second a month later, that one final.

She filled her green plastic watering can from an outdoor tap and stood on her tiptoes to water a hanging basket. Water dripped through the basket and onto the porch. In this heat it'd dry in no time.

She glanced at her watch. Another half-hour and she'd have to round up the boys for their weekly art lesson with Al across the street. Josh too. He'd probably been waiting down on Deloume for Matthew anyway. She still couldn't believe she'd talked them into it—well, Matthew really, the other two had just followed his lead as usual. Still, she figured some exposure to art would be good. And Al seemed happy to oblige—another nice surprise. After all, he was quite well known, at least on the island.

Andy emerged from the garage running, his shoelaces untied. A hummingbird zipped past her head and hovered for a moment beside a honeysuckle vine that had climbed up the porch railing, the bird's wings a blur, one of its tiny black eyes sizing her up, as if questioning her parenting. She looked back at the driveway but Andy had already gone too far to call after.

MATTHEW

He knelt beside the bent grass, the green pressed down in a metre-long oval.

"It's a deer bed," he said.

Josh nodded beside him, and Andy murmured behind. He studied his best friend and his brother as they looked at the flattened grass in awe. Josh standing tall and thick, dark hair, his brown eyes moving fast, as if he were afraid that by staring at any one thing he might miss something important. And next to him Andy, small and thin with white-blond hair and cornflower blue eyes, his T-shirt covered in grass stains and dirt from the fern spears.

Around them salal and underbrush grew high, and aside from the indentation of the deer's body in the grass before them, the forest surged upwards in tangles of green—the houses of Deloume Road out of sight completely.

"Where do you think the deer is?" asked Josh.

Matthew glanced at his friend's furrowed brow, a head higher than his own. "Miles away probably," he said, touching the grass to see if it was still warm. It wasn't, and there was no musty smell of piss either.

"Think it was a buck?"

"Maybe. The beds all kinda look the same though." He stood up and swung his stick in an arch, cutting nettles at the

31

waist, the stems folding over and hanging from their sticky green sinews. He'd seen a dead buck just yesterday in Bob Ford's truck. The truck had been parked at the end of the man's driveway and Matthew had stopped on his bike and taken a look. Bob had probably shot it himself for the antlers. The blood hadn't bothered him—but those open eyes, just staring. Too still to seem real.

The boys continued bushwhacking through the under-growth, knocking down stinging nettles and hook-thorned blackberry vines, Josh breaking sticks and twigs underfoot and stumbling every few steps, and Andy trying to walk and watch his feet at the same time, bumping into branches and giggling. At last they reached the massive clump of salmonberry bushes, the paper-wood stems twice as tall as them, the green leaves in full stretch, lush and bright. And countless red and orange ber-ries, each one like a cluster of glistening salmon roe.

He smiled at the other two.

"Lunchtime," he said.

JOSH

Juice frothed at the corners of his mouth as he chewed a handful of berries, sweet at first, then a hint of bitterness. He dug at the tiny seeds in his teeth with his tongue.

None of them spoke. There was a flutter in the thicket as a blue jay emerged from the leaves, ruffled its feathers and took flight, blue through the hanging branches and grey and brown bark.

"Wow, look at him go," he said.

"Faster than a speeding bullet," said Matthew. "My dad says you gotta pay fifty bucks if you kill one."

Josh thought about this for a moment, then plucked another berry from a branch overhead. "Good."

His friend smiled and Josh caught a glimpse of his perfect white teeth. Matthew was shorter than him, smaller, but somehow more put together, tidy. Even his reddish-brown hair stayed in place most of the time, while his own stuck sweaty to his forehead.

He'd almost cleaned out the branches around him and he wandered around the bushes slowly, stepping on the undergrowth and nettles, looking for the best place to pick berries without having to move much. He stumbled once over a branch but caught himself before he fell, looking over his shoulder to see if Matthew had noticed. His friend was out of sight. On the other side of the bush he found a small clearing with a flat stone in the middle. A break in the canopy of branches overhead allowed light to shine on the stone, and he crouched to look at what lay on the rock. At first it looked like a berry, small and round, dark red, but not quite right. Too smooth.

"Hey, come and take a look at this," he yelled.

Matthew crashed through the underbrush with Andy in tow.

"What do you think this is?" Josh pointed to the rock and the dime-sized reddish lump.

Matthew gestured to the red stains on the rock around the lump. "Blood," he said.

They stared at it for a moment in silence, Andy peering around them.

"Blood," said Andy. "Blood."

Matthew poked it once. "It's a stomach."

Josh stared at it and poked it once himself. "Sick."

ANDY

Light through the canopy. Bumblebee droning past his head
in bursts.

Fat bug.

Matthew poked the tiny stomach on the rock. Andy watched
his brother's finger, then looked at his own. Berry stains. Pink
on skin.

Voices, murmurs to words.

"A mouse?" asked Josh.

"Yeah, probably, or a newt," said Matthew. "Must have been
a weasel that killed it. They always leave the stomach. I guess it
doesn't taste good."

"Sick."

Andy laughed and the boys turned around. He spat out
some seeds and stuck out his tongue.

"Pink," he said, his mouth still open and his tongue hanging
out.

Josh laughed and stuck out his berry-stained tongue too.
Matthew started to say something but another bee zeppelined
by and Andy followed it back to the bush, humming so he could
feel his mouth vibrate. He picked a berry and rested it on his
tongue, imagining it painting the inside of his throat and stomach pink as he swallowed.

AL HENRY

The three boys sat outside on a huge piece of paper that he'd unrolled and taped to the deck. Andy was already covered in paint, but he'd arrived with berry stains all over his hands and face anyway, so Avril wasn't likely to be too sore. He watched them choose colours and brushes, Josh making a muck of things as usual. Not an artistic bone in the boy's body. But that wasn't really the point. He was there for Matthew. Hired muscle. A wing man. A necessary friendship.

Matthew was working on a landscape straight off. Ocean with a sun sinking behind it. Crude but bold. Bright colours. Clean strokes. The kid had something for sure. But then, Matthew seemed like the type of kid who was good at lots of things. His own son was the same way.

The afternoon heat was drying the paint quickly and the boys worked in silence. He saw Beth watching from the kitchen window. She smiled and pointed at Andy, who had dropped his brush and was using his fingers, so focused, so engrossed in his own little world. It was hard not to be jealous of that joy, that simple delight in the mere texture of materials.

The phone rang inside and he signalled to Beth that he'd get it, escape from the sun for a minute or two. He hurried to his study and picked up the receiver. The dispatch operator's voice trembled when he said hello, and Al knew right away that his son's plane had gone down.

He lowered himself into his chair. Carefully, he placed the heavy black telephone receiver on the surface of his desk. He laid his head beside it. The oak cooled his cheeks and his skin stuck to it. The arthritis in his wrist ached and spread, throbbing. He listened to blood pulsing in his temple for a moment, obscuring the thin voice of the dispatch operator calling his name, then lifted his head and hung up the phone.

A cardboard box sat open, spilling tiny metal staples onto the desk. He picked up a staple between his thumb and forefinger and placed it on the smooth surface in front of him. Then he picked up another and placed it beside the first. Then another. Then all of them, until part of his desk was covered with powder-silver metal. He smelled the grey metallic dust on his fingers and listened to the barking of the Fords' Doberman, to his own breathing.

He tried to see it, see the plane hit the forest, see the bent metal of his son's Single Otter scatter and become lost in dark evergreens and underbrush, as if that would make it easier, but all he could think about was the yellow toy plane his son had slept with as a child that still sat on a shelf in the spare room. His eyes blurred.

A plane's engine whined into a roar and napalm exploded in red bursts on the ridge of snow-covered trees ahead of him. Chinese soldiers rolled over the ground, ablaze and thrashing, trying to bury themselves in snow. The shouted order to let them burn. Save ammunition.

Hours after the battle they had dragged the smoking corpses into a shallow trench, covering the rows of bodies with snow and ruined tires. Above him on the hillsides, the imprints of the fallen were carved into the snow like twisted angels.

He forced his eyes to focus on his paintings—airplane after airplane on the walls. He'd sold so many now, and at least one to nearly every family in the neighbourhood. He could imagine his neighbours looking at them, men alone in their basements staring, half-empty bottles hanging from their hands. And the men's wives upstairs thinking about the paintings in the dead of night, wondering why their husbands couldn't express their sadness without anger, their grief without rage. Or maybe that was just how he saw them. The paintings on the wall were precise. The clouds looked like clouds and the airplanes were easy to identify—the markings and wingspans, everything was exact. But there was something about the action, about the implied movements in the paintings, that didn't quite convince. A wheel three inches from the runway, taking off or landing. Gear halfway up or down. The carmine glow of a sunrise about to crest the horizon, or the deep purple of dusk creeping into the edges of the canvas. Everything was suspended.

Beth walked into the room and looked at him.

"Who called?" she asked, twisting her silver wedding band with the forefinger and thumb of her right hand.

The muscles in his throat went taut and he couldn't speak. He watched the lines of her face and her grey hair becoming brush strokes. He blinked, and her flower-print blouse came back into focus. He ran his fingers over the surface of the desk, pushing the perfectly aligned staples to each side as he wrote his son's name through them. Beth leaned forward to see what he wrote but he swiped his hand across the desk, scattering the staples. The silence in the room became audible, filling the air between them.

"It's my son," he said finally, his own voice strange, the wrong tones. "It's Carson."

BETH

She left Al in his study and went and found the boys out front. Always the nurse first. Practical. Do this now, feel later.

"Sorry boys, but Al is a little sick. I'm afraid you'll have to head home."

She was surprised when her voice didn't crack.

Andy carried on mucking about, his hands blue and green, but Matthew put down his paintbrush and stood up.

"Is Mr. Henry okay?"

She felt herself tearing up but steadied herself on the deck's railing. "Could you make sure your brother gets home and cleaned up all right?"

Matthew nodded and he and Josh pulled Andy to his feet without touching the boy's paint-covered hands. It was a short walk home for them, and Beth watched them go, the two older boys out in front looking confused and Andy following behind, his green and blue hands out in front of him, as if he were letting the paint dry as he walked.

Jesus, she thought, and found herself wishing for an instant that she could escape with them. Instead, she picked up the paintbrushes and dropped them in a glass jar of water, feeling her finger and thumb stick to one. She looked around for a cloth to wipe her hands but her eyes filled with tears and she gave up and went inside.

No sound from Al's study, the house quiet and afternoon hot, and her standing in the kitchen with dread and worry making her stomach go all watery and her mouth dry, her fingers still stained with paint.

THE BUTCHER

Veins popped out on his wrists and forearms as he strained to keep the wheelbarrow from tilting. He pushed it slowly across the sun-stroked farm towards the graves, the wheel jarring and bumping over the rough, pig-dug earth.

Before him in the wheelbarrow lay a shovel and two dead piglets, runts, turning slightly blue now, the wisps of white hair on their bodies and ears stiff with a layer of dust. One of them had been crushed by its mother, a massive sow, seemingly unaware that she had rolled over her own offspring, breaking its tiny bones and pressing the air out of its lungs. The other had starved to death, outmuscled by its brothers and sisters. It was late in the year for it, but a runt was a runt.

The wheelbarrow bounced and tipped and the muscles in his shoulders burned to keep it straight. When he'd first started on the farm a sow had charged him, challenging him for her dead runt. He'd left the wheelbarrow and run, and the carcass had fallen out. The sow had sniffed it once then bit into its skull, crushing it in her massive jaws and grinding the bits of bone to swallow. He'd watched from a distance, terrified by how fast the fat, two-hundred-pound sow had moved. She had looked so docile and slow. Now he only buried pigs when the others were eating.

His father had told him stories of pigs tearing off farmers' legs, of sows so aggressive and territorial that they were renamed after demons. But as long as they kept giving birth each spring, they were too valuable to slaughter. And then there were the boars. He'd heard of one case where a boar's tusks hadn't been clipped in time, and it had run through the fields goring the stomachs out of cows, the bovines too slow to know what was happening until their intestines fell out in piles beneath them on the grass, the cows finally panicking when it was too late, running as a herd, treading and slipping on each other's organs.

He had sworn he wouldn't work like this forever. His father had tried so hard to keep him out of the slaughterhouses, to give him a better life. He'd even managed a few years of school. But now that he was in Canada, he couldn't shake the feeling he'd somehow taken a step backwards. Although the farm was hardly a slaughterhouse. And he didn't really mind the pigs. The longer he worked with them, the more he became convinced of their intelligence. They even covered themselves in mud on hot days so their skin didn't burn in the sun.

Could he have made more of himself? A teacher? Or a banker? He liked numbers and he was good at managing the money he had, however little.

He opened the gate near the end of the farm and passed through the fence that preventied the pigs from getting at the graves or mucking up the river beyond. He parked the wheelbarrow beside three mounds of earth, chose the one nearest and started digging, the blade of the shovel rasping through the dirt. He dug until he hit bone, then dumped the piglets in and covered them, the calluses on his hands hot with friction from the shovel's wooden handle. Sweat beaded on his forehead and the underarms of his shirt had soaked through.

He leaned on the shovel when he'd finished and looked up at the crows in the trees around the graves. He'd buried the pigs deep enough this time. Too deep for beaks and talons. A breeze started then stopped. He could just make out the faint trickle of the river, slight and summer slow, its water marking the end of the property. He dropped the shovel into the wheelbarrow and started back across the torn earth, where only thistle and broom grew in patches, and even then tentatively, as if aware that the pigs would tear them up no matter how deep their roots. As he walked back towards the barn there was a frantic flapping and rustle of leaves behind him as the crows dropped from the trees. They'd try to scratch their way down to where the runts lay, but it wouldn't work. Not this time.

For some reason this made him smile.

"Father, bless this food to good use in your servant's body. And give me patience. To wait for Maria and Petr. Keep them safe, Lord. Amen."

The bread wasn't fresh but it would do. He smiled as he bit and chewed. How quickly he'd become used to things he thought he'd never take for granted. The bread was only a day old, and he had cheese and ham—always ham. And milk from the dairy farm across Deloume. Not to mention a cupboard full of Campbell's soup cans.

He ate quickly but found that sitting at the wooden table alone caused his mind to wander. All day he busied himself with work, but in the evenings he couldn't pretend, couldn't block out the ongoing argument in his mind—the doubts he had about leaving his family behind, even though he told himself over and over that it was the only way.

After eating he showered and tried to wash the wet-iron smell of pig blood from his skin, lathering himself repeatedly with soap. When he stepped out of the shower and dried off, his skin felt taut and stretched, and it flaked slightly on his arms. He put on his pinstriped grey pyjamas and a pair of worn brown leather slippers that the Dutchman had left behind. He shuffled his feet on the carpet as he walked to his bedroom, pushing his toes into the ends of the slippers that were at least two sizes too large.

His bedroom was simple: a single bed covered by a Hudson's Bay Company wool blanket. And beneath that a white-turned-grey sheet, and a small flat pillow covered with an embroidered case. The hand stitching on the pillowcase was the work of his wife, and when he lay on his side and felt the raised flowers press into his face, he could almost convince himself he would wake next to her. He'd used the pillowcase to pad his suitcase when he'd left, and it was threadbare in patches.

The walls of the small room were white and stark, and the plaster was pockmarked. He imagined paintings hanging from the wall, though he wasn't sure why. The tiny holes were probably just made by nail hooks for coats and hats. The only interruption of white paint over plaster was a wooden cross, carved from pine and stained dark brown, which hung directly over the head of his bed. The cross was covered with tiny notches, one for each Sunday he woke alone. The notches had started long and deep but had become smaller each week. He would have lit candles but they were expensive, and he needed to save money for his family.

He had no bible in Ukrainian, and he'd all but given up trying to read it in English. He could understand many of the words but there was no rhythm in the English translation, or none that he could discern, as if whoever had translated it had forgotten the poetry of the Scriptures: the undulations of David's broken hallelujahs, and the richness of the Revelation. It was not what was written, but how. And to think people told him that his language sounded harsh. At least it had heart. Sam Toews, the dairy farmer across the road, liked to mimic his accent, smiling all the while and sounding, well, ridiculous really. It didn't bother him though. It was all in good fun.

His eyelids drooped and he yawned, his mind spinning quickly, then slower, then pausing on images: The face of his wife, her sun-kissed cheeks, curling brown hair, streaks of grey. A pale green sundress. Smooth brown ankles. Fields of clover and lavender. And the eyes of his son, deep brown, watching him.

Soon.

April, 1899

He sat in his tent with the flap open, listening to the rumble of thunder, rain drumming irregularly on the canvas.

The sky was starless.

Lightning forked over the bald mountain on the near horizon, illuminating the tall Douglas fir above him. He'd come surveying for the Royal Geological Society years back. Coal in Cumberland, Ladysmith and Nanaimo. Gold in Sooke. And rumours of copper and silver farther north and inland. But here it was all trees. Hundreds of feet tall. Pine, cedar, spruce and hemlock. Even the underbrush, the ferns and salal, grew ten feet high in places, and he had to stick mainly to deer trails and logging paths, looking for limestone and telltale signs of missed coal seams. So far he'd seen nothing worth taking out but lumber. Lord knew the railways needed ties. And the mill town on the water five miles distant spoke to this. Still, he found himself not wanting to leave.

The forest was thick and wet but not as dark as those farther west and north—the east coast of Vancouver's island drier in summer, with more sunlight finding its way through the canopy onto outcroppings of mossy volcanic rock and even occasional meadows of tall brown grass and wildflowers amongst Garry oaks, where he'd startled deer and elk. He could farm this land. This small valley, already partially logged. Although the spring rains this year were giving him pause. He'd grown up on a farm in Shropshire, back in England. Pastures for sheep and cows. God Almighty, how long would it take to clear space here for a farm like that? The massive tree above him would be downed soon he guessed. The land could be cleared all right, although it might take years, younger blood and a stronger back than his, and even then it'd be hell taking down the trees in numbers. How much dynamite would you need just for the stumps?

He'd been offered more money working with a crew felling giants but he was too old for that insanity, and he'd already seen too much. Seen the oxen dragging the massive trunks over muddy skids towards the sawmill on the coast. Seen a topper's tree split and crack on him, the top falling away but impaling him on shards of wood that shot out backwards. And the top had hung there by its sinews and bark, hundreds of feet up, threatening to fall at any moment, preventing anyone else from scaling the tree to bring the poor bastard down. So they'd left him up there for days, covered in a black cloud of insects and crows and vultures.

No, surveying was fine for now, and if he did anything else, it'd be to find his own land.

Three months in the wild this time out. Wintering in Victoria before that, with its streetcars and telegraph, its Chinese quarter a tangle of dark brick alleys, and all the sealers bored and restless for the spring and summer when the animals would migrate north past Vancouver Island to the Bering Sea, and they could take their pelts by the tens of thousands. But the city's clogged harbour lay a full thirty miles south over mountains now, and he was alone. He visited logging camps occasionally, or the town around the sawmill when he needed supplies or drying out, but for the most part he worked by himself. He wasn't lonely though. In his spare time he catalogued birds and insects. His notebooks were full of sketches but so far he hadn't found anything new. Botanists and naturalists had explored the island already—bloody Douglas had attached his name to damn near everything that moved or grew. As a boy he'd spent as much time outside as possible, fascinated by insects and birds. He'd dreamed of new discoveries, inventing nonsensical Latin names for them. *Arachnid delouminia. Gerardus orinthnus.* There had always been something about the watchful eyes of the Shropshire woods that had made him feel taken care of, or at least in company. And it was true here too. The birds were aware of him, curious but not afraid. And they weren't just small birds like swallows and grey jays, but bald eagles, red-tailed hawks and turkey vultures. And the massive ravens, their wings beating out a sound like wind through cracked mortar, so distinct he'd first thought he was hearing the descent of an angel, Gabriel come to speak into the wilderness. All those secret words. All those lost names. He could feel it. The rocks and trees and soil, each fish-eye huckleberry permeated with a force, with a power—the Lord God's resonance, shock waves of Creation, of the day the island was snapped off the continent by the divine hand and set adrift in the Pacific.

Lightning cracked open the black jar of night. He closed his eyes and saw the flash again and again. His pulse pounded in his temples. Time seemed to slow, become clumsy, his arms goosebumping in the hush after the thunderclap.

A lightning bolt struck the Douglas fir high above him, sending sparks, ash and burning pine needles through the rain down around his tent. He stood up, unable to look away as branches cracked and fell. He shook himself fully awake and swatted at a spark on his tent. Burning pine needles singed his arms as he tore up tent pegs and hauled his shelter into the wet underbrush away from the tree. Around him flaming branches cast moving shadows and tiny fires in trees and ferns hissed in the rain.

MILES FORD

He sat in the highest of the three metal pipes that ran beneath Deloume Road so the river could pass freely underneath. The pipes were stacked in a pyramid with two at the base, the top one dry all summer and just large enough for him to crouch or sit inside without ducking, its ends covered by roots hanging down and ferns growing up. He liked this spot. He could listen to Matthew and Josh talk while they fished or lazed by the river, but today he sat alone, memories of the boys' voices whispering around and around the metal in faint echoes.

"God's real, my mom said so," came Josh's voice first.

"You can't know it though," said Matthew.

"Maybe I do."

"Liar."

A car passed on the road above, the pipe vibrating. He imagined the vehicle carrying Katie and Elaine to a friend's house somewhere near Mill Bay, maybe close to where his brother lived. He never played with the girls from a few houses up the road, but everything they had was new. Even their house. And their car was a shiny red Honda. Not like his dad's truck, old and rusting. Black. His dad said foreign cars were garbage. That they were unreliable. But his dad's truck always needed repairs, and it was getting so old it looked like it might not even be able to make it into Mill Bay soon.

He'd walked into town alone once. It'd taken him all day. He'd told himself he'd gone for no reason, but deep down he'd hoped to see his brother. His dad and brother didn't get along, and he only saw him a few times a year. But he was almost ten years older than Miles anyway, so it wasn't like they could really talk or anything. Same with his sister in Nanaimo. Mill Bay hadn't been busy when he'd got there but there'd been more people than on Deloume, all of them shopping for groceries or hardware, or eating in the town's small diner. He hadn't seen his brother and no one had paid any attention to him, as if he belonged there. Or maybe they had just been ignoring him. Like Matthew and Josh did.

Whispers along dark metal, through the loose-change smell of pipe and earth.

"You have to bait the hook."

"I'm not trying to catch anything."

"What are you fishing for then?"

"I dunno. Just feel like doing something."

"You should bait it."

He wished they'd come to the river today so he could listen to them talk, even about people he'd never seen. Sometimes he felt like he knew the people they talked about, what they looked like, how they smelled, the sounds of their voices. And he liked watching Andy. The way he didn't talk much but always noticed things. Like when Matthew and Josh were fishing, Andy would be staring at a rock, as if he were trying to read the surface. He was retarded, but not like other kids he'd seen. No drooling or anything scary. He just acted like he was in his own world. And all the counting was kind of funny.

It was cool in the pipe and Miles spoke into the musty air.

"Miles," he said.

And the pipe said it back to him in a rasping whisper.

Another car rumbled over the river, maybe Matthew and Andy's dad's blue Toyota Corona. He wondered where their dad worked. Not in Mill Bay. There wasn't enough there, and he always wore a shirt and tie. He probably worked in one of the big cities on the island—Victoria or Nanaimo.

There was never any junk outside Matthew and Andy's house. It was the closest home to his trailer and sometimes he'd sneak through the trees between their properties to see it, with its dark-stained wood siding and mowed lawn out front. It made the old refrigerators and tires outside his place seem so ugly. And his trailer so small and plain. He didn't want to go back there now. The Doberman would be waiting for him, just sitting all chained up, watching the driveway. What good was a dog you couldn't play with? And all that junk. Just a big pile of nothing.

He'd heard Matthew and Josh talking about it.

"It's mostly just crap."

"Yeah, half of it's all rusted out."

"My dad says none of it's worth nothing. And most of it's stolen."

Sometimes when the boys left he'd repeat what he could remember of their conversations, listening to his own soft voice, the words catching and cracking in his throat.

He shifted in the pipe, peering out through the roots and ferns. Below him water dribbled into the pool from the lower pipes, the movement barely visible, a slow stirring.

Maybe they weren't coming today. He looked over his shoulder through the long pipe to the dim light at the other end.

"Miles," he said, listening as the metallic echo faded and disappeared.

SAM TOEWS

He stared at the padlock hanging open on the gate. Had he done it, or had it been one of his hired hands? Wouldn't have been the first time. Kids were hard workers but most of them had the minds of fence posts. In any case, one of the cows was missing. He only hoped she'd wandered down Deloume towards the river and houses and not the other way onto Shawnigan Mill Bay Road.

A year ago a heifer with calf had wandered off Deloume and been hit by a logging truck. The eighteen-wheeler had knocked the cow clear over the ditch. The driver had radioed the police. Nothing more he could've done. And the police had called him to get rid of the dead animal. Fair enough. He'd found the cow lying with her back broken, spine hyperextended and belly split open, the unborn calf half out in a pile of intestines and blood and God knew what else. He'd had to pay one of his hands over-time to help him load the damn thing into his truck and bury her. Whole thing had cost him a small fortune.

He shut and locked the metal gate behind him, walking quickly at first then slowing when the butcher waved to him from the pig farm across the road. Sam tipped the brim of his baseball cap in acknowledgement. He walked over and leaned on the wire fence, his hands between barbs.

"Seen a cow wander past by any chance?" he asked when the butcher was close enough.

The butcher shook his head. "Sorry. I just came out."

"Thanks anyway," said Sam. "Pigs okay?"

"Always the same," said the butcher, smiling, his white teeth crooked.

Sam nodded. "That's the truth."

He pushed off the wire fence and said goodbye. The man smiled again and wished him luck.

The butcher was all right. Worked hard. Plus he was generous with his ham. But there was something about a man living alone with all those pigs. And the accent wasn't always easy. Course, he lived alone too, and he wasn't no nightingale himself. He continued down the road, watching for cow shit along the sides or on the gravel. Damn cow. How had she known the fence was unlocked? And probably only for a couple of hours.

A car glided past and two small girls in the back seat turned to look at him. Katie and Elaine from up the road. Katie stuck out her tongue. Little rascal.

He walked over the river, listening for the trickle. He paused. A murmur from the trees around him. Faint. He couldn't make out the words though. He walked to the side of the road and stared down at the river but couldn't see anyone. But he could still hear it, a quiet voice, as if it were coming up from underground. Or was it just the movement of water?

He shrugged it off and kept walking. It wasn't a cow, that was sure. He passed the stop sign and saw her standing on the side of the road in the shade, eating tall grass that grew in swaths along the edge of the ditch.

"So," he said. "You couldn't have done that at home?"

The cow rolled an eye and continued chewing, a black-and-white newspaper comic against the green backdrop of trees.

"Well I guess you're not going to explain yourself," he said, searching the ditch for a suitable branch in case the cow needed some encouragement finding her way back to the farm. "At least you walked in the right direction."

The cow raised her head, ears twitching off flies. A pile of wet shit dropped onto the road.

He chuckled. "I'm sure the neighbours will appreciate it," he said, patting the animal's neck and turning her towards the farm.

IRENE

She placed her cup of persimmon tea on the coffee table and put her warm hands on her belly. The child kicked. Her fingers were swollen and her wedding ring pinched tight. She'd have to take it off soon, while she still could. She leaned back against the wall and wiggled her hips to adjust the cushion on the floor beneath her, bumping the wooden rocking chair next to her with her knee. She imagined trying to sit in the chair, how the peg joints would creak and groan beneath her weight.

"With child" was a phrase that had made her laugh when she'd first heard it. She listed the other words she knew—*pregnant, expecting*—and wondered why there wasn't a word that meant all of them. In English there were so many words that meant the same thing, but few of them ever seemed to quite express anything right. Or was that just because she couldn't associate the meanings with herself? Foreign words beading off her skin like water.

Photos of her family were thumbtacked to the living room wall and several of the pictures had started to roll up from the bottom. They were vulnerable to passing time too, changing just like the people they showed, just like her. Her mother had called again yesterday offering to send her a plane ticket home. For her to keep safe until the baby was born. It was too risky to fly now but her mother wasn't giving up that easily. Already thinking about the future. Planning.

Eight months pregnant. Had it really been that long since she'd arrived in Canada? How long then since it had happened? Two months since the call. Since that man with his news-anchor voice had told her about Joseph. And she'd just stood there silently, holding the phone, trying to make sense of what he was telling her, of the words he'd used that she hadn't realized until partway through the conversation meant "*dead*."

She needed her husband so badly now. She tried to talk to Beth and Avril, both a few houses down, but it wasn't the same. Avril was usually too busy with her boys for more than a few quick words, and Beth was wonderful to her but she was thirty years older. She and Al had asked her and Joseph over when they'd first moved to Deloume, but she'd shied away from invites, worried that her English wasn't good enough, and still not quite able to believe that dinner at someone's home could be casual. In Korea, only family members ate at each other's homes unless it was a special event, and even then . . . She wondered if she'd offended Al by not going over. The few times they'd spoken he'd seemed distant and cold. Beth had told her he could be like that, and that it had nothing to do with her, but she wasn't convinced. She'd also said he'd fought in Korea forty years ago, but Irene hadn't found the courage to ask him about it yet. He almost looked Korean, his skin darker than Beth's. A Native. What did that mean here?

After it had happened, Beth had started coming over. Avril too every now and again, sometimes with her youngest, Andy. They were so kind. Still, it was all such a far cry from sitting with her friends on the grass outside her university classrooms in Busan. Cherry trees and ginkgos—the familiar blossoms and that hint of humidity in the late spring air. All of them giggling with excitement over her dating a Canadian, even if his family was Korean. And a career soldier—how romantic. She missed the ease of it. Gossiping and telling stories. She remembered telling her friends how she and Joseph had met. How he'd been in Busan for a war memorial ceremony at the UN cemetery. She'd been on her way to visit her mother and he'd been standing with a group of soldiers. They were off duty but she knew how to spot a foreign soldier. Not that it was hard. Short hair. White skin. Louder than a loud city. Busan was full of them on weekends.

The group Joseph had been with was the same. It was early evening but they were already drunk. Celebrating what? Freedom for a night? They had spilled out of a bar and onto the sidewalk, and were harassing passersby. She had thought about crossing the street but for some reason she'd tried to walk past. One of the soldiers had grabbed her arm and slurred something through paint-thinner breath. Joseph had stepped in gently, turned the soldier away from her and then smiled back over his shoulder. It had surprised her at the time because he looked Korean, and locals knew better than to mess with soldiers. Technically they were under control, with the MPs and all of the restrictions on behaviour that came with being in the military. But it didn't always work the way it was supposed to and things often got out of hand.

She'd told her friends that she never would have stopped if she hadn't been so surprised. Joseph had spoken to the soldier in English then apologized to her in Korean. He didn't speak well, but between her English and his Korean they'd managed.

Later, when she'd moved here, before he'd been assigned to the Gulf and shipped out, he'd insisted they speak English with each other, but he had weighed his words so carefully, and searched so patiently for ones she would understand, that she had talked to him with almost that same ease, without hesitating or panicking when she couldn't find the perfect word. He'd listened well too, tried to understand why she'd been terrified of walking alone on the road here. She'd got over it eventually, but it had seemed so quiet and isolated at first. Eerie. And then the surprises had come. She translated the word into English. Perhaps *surprises* wasn't the right word. It suggested birthday parties or practical jokes. But pregnancy? And then Joseph?

She sighed, her breath hot from the tea, and stood up slowly, her pelvis loose and her balance shaky. She walked to the bathroom and looked in the mirror. Her skin was darker than it had been in Korea. No whitening cream or sun umbrellas here. And her thin eyebrows were real now, less arched than the ones she used to draw on. She frowned at a single strand of grey hair and considered pulling it out.

Her husband's voice came to her then, teaching her simple rhymes and songs: *One for sorrow*.

She wondered how he'd look at her now. Her belly had grown so much in such a short time. A flutter of panic started in her chest and moved up to her throat, and she swallowed and breathed deeply, trying to avoid thinking about everything that had happened. If only he would come home and tell her it had all been a mistake, the phone call, the newspapers, everything, and instead show her a scar she could trace with her fingers.

She took another deep breath, staring into her own eyes in the mirror until they went out of focus and she blinked. She flexed her back and the baby kicked, not hard though, just a reminder. She spotted another grey hair.

Two for joy.

She peed and washed her hands, then returned to the living room, to her wooden rocking chair. Even though she couldn't make herself comfortable in it, she loved the honey-stained oak, how it was fitted together with wooden pegs instead of nails and screws. Sunlight streamed through branches and the sliding glass door onto the room's hardwood floor. The baby kicked again, this time harder. She sat down on the square red cushion and stared out the window into the prism dawn. Sun dogs danced through cedars and steam rose from dew-covered branches. As she stared the light took shape in the boughs: a face watching her. A cloud passed over the low sun and the wet light disappeared. And the branches were branches and the light was dull, bruised and tired.

AL HENRY

He woke with a headache, rolled over, swallowed two Aspirin and lay in bed until the throbbing in his temples subsided. The house was quiet. Beth was probably out shopping. He'd seen her crying in the kitchen before they'd gone to bed. With the tap running so he wouldn't notice.

He stared up at the ceiling's white stucco.

The phone call of the day before seemed ancient and sharp all at once. Not much information yet. It was impossible to know how long it'd take to find the plane. Carson had been flying medical supplies to a leper colony near the Alaskan border. Just the idea of it sounded foreign, like something from a history textbook, but his son had flown there before. There weren't many colonies left. The one up north was pretty big though, and there were doctors and nurses. But it was isolated, and windfall often blocked the access roads.

"God's country," his son had said. "Although they say you can see some of the clear-cuts from space. Whole fucking valleys and ranges stripped bare."

God's country.

Hadn't thought much about God for a long time. Not since Korea maybe. And before that his mother's stories. Maybe he should have passed those on to his son. It wasn't like they taught them in schools. The old gods. Raven, Raccoon, Seagull. At least it would have been something. His first wife would have liked that. Maybe she wouldn't have left him to go back to the reserve. His mother would have liked it too.

Flights so far north were always tough, and the landings were pretty much hell. Runways in bush pilot country were just rough-cleared fields or potholed strips of disused logging road. But his son put his plane down on them. Over and over. The staff of the colony had cleared the landing strip this time with extra care because of a windstorm a few days before, but his plane hadn't shown up. The last radio contact had been about an hour before that. He might have survived the crash, but that was only half the battle. Someone had to find him. And once they found him, they had to figure out a way to get him out. There was too much forest for helicopters to cover. The only hope was that he'd gone down close to the colony or a logging camp and could hike out.

Again he tried to see it happen. He sat in the cockpit with his son, watched the trees growing as the plane descended, lights flashing on the dashboard. The last radio call, and then a second of gracefulness before sky became treetops.

How long would it take them to find the plane? Hours? Days? He'd heard stories of loggers finding plane wrecks in trees, skeletons picked clean in the cockpit by birds and insects, seat belts still intact.

God. Not Carson.

He couldn't swallow. He tried to tell himself his son knew the risks. And his boy was one hell of a pilot. Could land a Single Otter on water with floats or on snow with skis. He'd said that sometimes he even let air out of his tires so he could land on makeshift runways over rocks and small logs.

As the Aspirin numbed his muscles he leaned over and picked the newspaper up off the bedside table. Anything to help him stop thinking about Carson. He opened the paper at a random page, the comics, studying the strips until colour shot through his irises and swirled, blending with memory.

Burning pages of cartoons wheeling in the wind, sticking to blood-soaked clothing and pieces of men and women that were scattered through the snow, frozen blue. Around him ash and snowflake became one, and heat from the fires and cold air off the mountains buffeted him from all sides.

Comic books. Of all the damn things to find on the front lines. Americans too full of themselves, too ready to supply their troops with entertainment. But no one had been ready for the North. For the mountains. For so many dead and maimed. By the time he'd arrived in Korea with the Princess Patricia Light, so much had happened, so much slaughter on both sides. Before he'd shipped out he'd thought the Americans would stroll through the peninsula. Just push the gooks right up into China, or Siberia. They'd already broken out of the Busan perimeter in the far south, MacArthur's Inchon landing taking the enemy by complete surprise, and he'd reckoned Canadian soldiers like him were just along for the ride. Stupid. His first taste of mortars raining down from the hills around Miryang had put an end to those thoughts once and for all. Daegu and Seoul had been blown to rubble, and in February of '51 his battalion started to lose numbers as they headed into the Kapyong valley. Then the Chinese engaged and everything changed again.

Carson had asked him about Korea when he'd still been in school and they'd talked about it. Some of it. Crazy old

MacArthur in his Tokyo tower, people lining up outside with gifts, worshipping him like a god, when all the General had done was fuck everything up in Korea. But Carson hadn't been content with the politics. He'd wanted to know how it had felt.

Cold. That had been the worst thing. Strange, he'd seen children burn to death, women raped, thousands buried in shallow graves, but it was the cold that he remembered. The way it tore at his face day and night.

He stood calf-deep in the snow, warming his hands on a burning supply truck. They'd pushed north through Seoul again, almost to the Kansas Line. His detachment of Patricias had joined the Royal Australian Third and they'd left behind a group of Royal Engineers. Despite the crap of the daily grind, the Engineers' ingenuity had astounded him. He'd seen them make bridges out of burnt-out railcars and repair roads at almost the same pace the army could move. It was slow going without them. All day streams of women and children and scatterings of old men passed him in each direction. Once a group of shorn-headed monks had marched by, wearing their dried-orange-peel robes outside of other layers, so that each of them looked obese, like derelict Buddhas waddling south, probably leaving behind a bombed-out temple in the hills.

Refugees from the South headed North. Refugees from the North headed South.

Above him loomed the mountains, snow-covered, with short pines and tangled underbrush crystallized in the cold. Somewhere ahead of them an army waited. Stragglers and deserters, the commanders told them. Didn't feel right though. Word down the line was that ambushes were happening more often, that the American First and Ninth divisions had withdrawn and that the entire ROK Sixth was in full retreat. Had to be the Chinese. Orders were to make hill 677 ASAP. Why the hell couldn't they find this army?

A plane overhead. Beside him a Korean boy stopped in his tracks and pointed. His dirty face was peeling in red patches. But his eyes lit up for a second. All this crap and death but just for a second ... Al stopped too and watched the F-51 Mustang bank right and disappear over the broken white teeth of the mountain range. A woman grabbed the boy and dragged him on, scolding.

That night he sat awake in a tent canteen, wrapped in as many blankets as he could find. The Aussies across the crate table had given up on cards, the air too cold for their bare fingers.

A shadow at the tent flap. They were well inside the perimeter and it was unlikely that anyone could have got through. All the same, he reached for his rifle.

A woman leaned into the light, Korean, her face and lips chapped, skin cracked and flaking.

"How the hell'd she get in here?" asked one of the Aussies.

"Piss off," said another, waving her away.

The woman shifted her gaze to Al. The light from the lantern played off her black eyes, turning them liquid, mercury, alive. She was wrapped in a few layers, not enough though, and her hair was already frozen. He could have reached out and broken off strands.

"Mul," she stammered. Then again, louder. *"Mul."*

"I told you to get lost," said the Aussie. "Can't carry every bloody gook in the country, can we?"

The other Aussie turned his back on the woman but she didn't seem to notice, instead inching closer to where Al sat.

"*Mul juseo.*"

"I don't speak . . ." Al paused and shook his head. "I don't know."

A South Korean soldier ducked his head in the tent, muttered something and dragged the woman out. The whole thing only took a minute.

"Don't sweat it," said one of the men across the table. "She probably wanted something for sex. A ride home. Fucking desperate, that's all."

Desperate.

In the morning they'd started moving north again, slowly, sometimes on foot, watching the hills, surveillance planes above. Not far from camp they passed an abandoned cart. As he walked closer, he saw it wasn't empty. Pairs of frozen bare feet hung over one edge. And inside, stacked like ammunition, were row on row of bodies—at least a dozen of them, frozen solid, their shoes and coats gone, a light layer of snow over them in patches. His eyes rested on a woman's face, chalk white, eyes open. It was her. A magpie landed on the edge of the cart, hopping onto the woman's shoulder. He turned away.

"Ain't a pretty sight," said one of the soldiers behind him. "Hard to believe I'm getting used to it."

Al nodded.

They made tracks side by side through the hard snow, the crusted surface breaking with each step, the edges cutting at their shins and calves.

"Speak any Korean?" asked Al.

"Only a little. Got a book when they told me I was shipping out. Haven't read much though."

"Any idea what *mul* means?"

"Sure, that's easy. Means 'water.'"

He shook himself and blinked. He'd scrunched up the newspaper. He folded it shut and smoothed it so Beth could read it later. The front page announced the August air show at the Comox air force base four hours up-island. Carson had loved the show as a boy. F-4 Phantoms, B-52s, F-51 Mustangs. They used to take out library books about airplanes, jets, helicopters and space shuttles. Not picture books but scientific journals and encyclopedias, tomes with titles about the history of flight and the heroes of aviation. Charles Lindbergh, Guy Gibson, Chuck Yeager. Aerodynamics became a secret language between them, and when Al painted an airplane his son would study it for hours, and they'd talk over the details of lift and airflow, fuel requirements and runway space.

Once, after he had painted a Canadair water bomber, his son had asked him why his paintings were so sad. It was the first time that anyone had told him his paintings weren't happy, that they evoked anything other than a twinge of excitement at seeing a plane in flight. And it had bothered him ever since that his work might be capable of causing sorrow. He'd never been able to answer the question. But now he wondered if he'd somehow known all along, if some intuition or paternal instinct had told him all those years ago that the airplanes his son loved would kill him.

———

He drank coffee as he sat at his easel. It was the first time in years that painting hadn't come easily. He'd never really thought about it before, just like he never thought about getting sick when he wasn't. For nearly four decades he'd sat in front of white surfaces and known exactly what he wanted them to look like when he was done painting. But as he glanced around the studio at his finished work, he couldn't imagine that they'd ever been blank canvases, and the clean white before him on the easel reminded him of a freshly painted wall. Too pure to spoil with that first nail.

A dog barked on Deloume Road, and he realized that he was waiting for the phone to ring, that his ears were straining into the silence, the house quiet, as if hushed, the walls and carpets listening to him listen.

BETH

She sat beside Avril on the woman's front porch, her hands shaking as if to spite the mantra running through her head: *stay strong, stay strong . . .*

"They haven't found the plane yet, but . . ." She let her voice trail off and Avril leaned over to rub her back.

"I'm so sorry Beth. I wish there was something we could do."

Beth forced a smile. She and Avril had never been very close, in part because she was twenty years older and had only lived on Deloume for a few years, but their houses were right across the street from one another, and the woman was easy to like. And she couldn't very well go and cry all over Irene. God knew the poor girl had enough on her plate. She was still practically a child herself. Younger than Al's son even.

"I don't know how to act. I've never seen Al like this. Not even when his mother died. He wouldn't even talk about it last night, not that I blame him, but—what am I supposed to *do*?"

They sat without speaking. Thank God Avril was staying quiet. No advice. No silly little sayings. Just twisting a curling lock of hair in her free hand, winding it tightly around her fingers. Her hair had all but fallen out of a knot onto her pale neck, the auburn strands mixed with grey. Her face was freckled slightly from months of summer and she wasn't wearing any makeup. Was she thinking about what it would be like to lose one of her own kids? Beth caught herself as her mind swung from panic and worry to the regular. The normal. Avril's hair. Makeup. How could she just sit there thinking these things while Al was home alone, sick with fear and anxiety? She stood up. She had to pull it together. They just had to wait. Wait until they knew. Stay strong.

The Stop Sign

A cloud drifts over the sun as we stand in silence. Dragonflies that have paused to bake in the heat lift off from the cracked edges of the road, and my eyes have to adjust to see them. All at once the cloud passes and the dragonflies become insect oil slicks, stutter-buzzing above, their translucent wings shimmering as they disappear down the road.

"Time seems kinda slow here," I say. "Did you ever notice that?"

We leave the road and walk through the grass past the crabapple trees to the edge of the dairy farm, where cattle stand or lie in groups. Swarms of flies dodge their pendulum tails and twitching ears. The cows are encouraged to stay at home by a mixture of wooden fencing and electric wiring. I lean against one of the posts. It's not hard to keep cows, but the gates are important. Some farmers insist cows have a sixth sense for unlocked gates and will instinctively wander out of their pasture whenever possible. The same farmers talk about how eerie it is, how the cows never move faster than a meandering shuffle, how they seem to have no intention or ambition at all, and yet slip out of pastures like slow-moving clouds.

"I like them," I say, nodding at the cows. "They never hurt anybody."

The cows lean on each other, vying for position and jostling for space beneath the few trees that shade the dry earth. They're loud now, complaining about the heat, moaning and blinking off flies.

I break off the top of a long piece of grass and grind the wheat-like head between my thumb and forefinger. The pasture has bare spots that have been grazed over and trampled to dust, where weeds prosper among cow-pies. Huge bushes of Himalayan blackberry grow tall and dense throughout the field, with paths through them that cows have cut in their lumbering way. The rich smells of manure and overripe blackberries float on heat waves and all at once the stench seems unbearable.

"I didn't mean for it to happen," I say. "We were just kids."

You look away and I follow your eyes to a purple butterfly marionetting its way into a patch of blackberry vines, its fluttering visible for a moment between branches before it disappears altogether into the dusty lost sunlight.

You turn your back on me and return to the road, then walk to the old stop sign. You reach down to pick up a stone, but pause. A dog trots down Deloume, its tongue hanging from its long jaw, its mangy and patchy dark brown fur full of burs. One of its ears is bent and flops down but the other is pointy. It pauses at the stop sign and sniffs the wooden pole, then lifts its hind leg before carrying on.

I stare at the weathered metal octagon, find myself trying to count scratches, rock scars. Like trying to count stars. The bullet hole through the O had been small at first, but over time it had rusted and the edges had curled back until it was large enough to throw a rock through. At three-thirty on school days the clang of stone on metal used to ring down the length of

Deloume. I threw hundreds of rocks. Made wishes when I got one through.

I wonder if you see it the way I do now. How it's bolted to a wooden four-by-four, not a metal pole like they usually are these days, and how the wood's painted white and there are names, phone numbers and pictures drawn or scratched all over its surface. The white paint has cracked along the grain of the wood as it expands with the summer heat, and grass patches out in a rough circle from the base, where one small daisy grows, yellow in the middle with white petals, each one with touches of pink.

I want to tell you about how I used to pick daisies and pull off their petals for "she loves me not," but there is something about the pink shading on the flowers that reminds me of it. Of water tainted with blood.

MATTHEW

He stood in the backyard and held the dry, Saran-wrap skin of the garter snake in one hand, careful not to crush it. He tried to imagine what it would feel like to shed his own skin all at once and he pinched his arm, then looked around to see if anyone was watching. He'd told Josh he wanted to play alone for a while, and Andy was off somewhere by himself too. He put the skin down on the grass and clover at his feet. Mr. Henry had once told him something about finding a snakeskin, about it being a sign of change. He looked at his house, at the sliding glass door into the kitchen, the window of his parents' bedroom, and up to the TV antenna, a metal tree growing out of the roof shingles.

Nothing had changed. Not yet. Maybe the snakeskin didn't mean anything. Maybe it just was. He walked away from the back of his house down the path towards the well in the forest. He named trees as he walked, remembering what his dad had taught him: dogwood, red alder, pine and more. The tree limbs closed into a canopy overhead and the early afternoon sun scattered into beams through leaves onto the path ahead of him. It was a relief to walk through the forest without having to fend off stinging nettles and thorns, and his legs felt light and loose. But without Josh or Andy around he didn't have to make it a game. Didn't have to run or hide if he didn't feel like it.

Less sunlight reached the forest floor around the sealed cement top of the shallow well, and the ground was marshy and damp. Thick green grass grew in limp patches and skunk cabbage that smelled of rotten vegetables sprouted from the mud, wet moss and decaying leaves.

The Fords' property to his right was marked by a rope strung from tree to tree, with laminated yellow and black No Trespassing signs hanging at random. Stupid. It was all just forest. Most of the plastic-coated signs had wrinkled and bent with age. The slack rope disappeared in places beneath the underbrush, and as his eyes followed the line he saw a flash of orange paint through green. It was the car. He checked that he was alone again before stepping over the rope and creeping towards the tangle of rusted orange metal, arms out to keep spiders' webs off his face.

He'd seen the car before but he'd never dared explore it in case the Fords let their Doberman off its chain. He was trespassing, but he hadn't seen the dog running free in weeks.

"How did you get here?" he asked the car, making his way around the dilapidated vehicle to the doorless passenger side. If he were Miles, he'd be out here playing in it all the time. But he never saw Miles anywhere except on the road.

He looked over the vehicle. It might have been a sports car once. All four tires were gone, as were the hood and trunk, and ferns were growing up through the engine. On the back, just above where the bumper should have been, was a discoloration in the shape of *TR6*.

Even metal can become forest, he thought, as he peered into the open frame. The glove compartment was still shut and he tried turning the tiny handle. It was locked or stuck. He reached underneath the compartment to see if it had rusted or rotted out but found only stinging nettles that had grown up though gaping holes in the floorboards. He stood up and sucked his fingers to ease the burning.

He walked back to his house slowly, trying to figure out how to pick the lock. He'd tried to unlock his parents' bedroom once with a small piece of wood kindling that had broken off inside the handle. Luckily his parents had assumed it was Andy, and he sure wasn't gonna come clean. It wasn't like Andy ever got in trouble anyways.

What he needed now was a key.

ANDY

He held his breath and sat still, holding the rope tight and allowing the backyard tire swing to slow. Matthew hadn't seen him. He watched his brother walk down the path. He'd seen how he had cradled the snakeskin, laid it gently on the grass. Andy closed his eyes. Garter snake crawling back into its skin. Twisting and writhing.

Be careful.

The swing was almost motionless now. He looked up the yellow fibres of the rope to where their braids wrapped around the giant tree arm. The rope had rubbed through the bark, and lumps of grey skin on the branch curled over each side of it.

Swallowing it.

For a moment after the swing stopped he felt the momentum.

Fast. Be careful.

He got off the swing, stumbled to his knees, then stood up and walked to where his brother had left the snakeskin on the grass. He picked it up and held it to his nose. Musty. His mom and dad's bedroom in the morning. On the skin were the slight imprints of scales, flaky and transparent. He carried it to the small sandbox beside the swing. The box was littered with uncovered cat crap and half-buried toy cars. He picked up a handful of sand and let it slide through his fingers, and even when his hand was empty he stared at it for a moment, trying to memorize the patterns of dust on his palm.

He dug a hole in the centre of the square box and put the snakeskin in it, counting the corners of the box before filling in the sand, as if marking the place on a map.

"Four," he said.

He looked down the path that his brother had taken just moments before.

Stop following me.

He brushed the sand off his hands. On his left thumb a hangnail had started, and the skin was peeling away from the cuticle towards his knuckle.

AVRIL

B ob Ford scanned their garage: wire fencing, tangles of Christmas lights with bulbs missing, boxes of shingles. She watched him sizing up the tools hanging on the wall, then their old lawn mower, its orange cord wrapped around it like a cartoon snake.

"That might need to go too," she said, nodding. "The tools are David's though. They stay."

Bob grunted. He was a thick man, with receding ash-coloured hair. His forearms were heavy, the hair on them wiry and covered in grease.

"We're not looking for much money, but it'd be great to get rid of some of it." Her voice came out strained, tentative. It was always the same talking to Bob. The way he looked right through her. Acted like she was nothing. She wished David were home from work.

One corner of the garage was stacked with boxes and paper bags of nails and screws and other odds and ends—leftovers from building the place a decade ago. Ten years and they still couldn't park in their own garage. But now that the boys were a little more independent she was running out of excuses. And God knew David wasn't going to get to it any time soon.

"David says the wire fencing's in good shape still. I haven't

checked it myself. We use it for keeping deer out of the garden," she added. "Although we usually string a line above it too.
Amazing how high they can jump."

"Pigs' blood works fine," said Bob, sniffing and wiping his
nose on the shoulder of his shirt.

"Sorry?"

"Pigs' blood. In the soil. You mix it in. Deer won't go near it."

"Really? That's . . ."

Horrible, she thought.

"Fifty bucks for the lot."

She looked over the garage again, her eyes resting on a rust-
flecked Christmas tree base. They'd bought a potted one last
year and then planted it. No need for a stand. Needles everywhere, but it'd been worth it just for the smell of pine inside for
a week or two. It'd been their first Christmas without her mom,
and her dad hadn't come out from Alberta for it. First time for
that too. They hadn't even talked.

"Maybe I could go sixty, but it's gonna take a while for me to
clear it out," said Bob. "Labour ain't free."

"No," she said, fixing her eyes on the man's dirty hands. "It
wouldn't be, would it?"

He sniffed again.

She thought about asking if he'd heard about Al's son but
hesitated, nervous about what he might say. She could imagine
him going off about Indians belonging on reserves. Like something her father might . . . In any case, Bob didn't talk to Al or
Beth much, at least not to her knowledge, so it wasn't really her
place to tell him. The Fords kept mostly to themselves except
for interactions like this. Business. That was just their way. It
made her feel sorry for Miles though. Missing school all the

time. No friends she'd ever seen. And she couldn't seem to talk Matthew into spending time with him.

"You know, I've been meaning to ask you, how old is Miles? I know he doesn't go to school with Matthew, but he's the same age, isn't he?"

Bob cleared his throat, glancing again at the lawn mower. She watched his lips move silently, like a child's counting pennies. David had bought a new gas-powered mower that spring. No electrical cord to trip over or risk tangling in the blades, he'd said. And it'd be easier for Matthew to learn on. Harder to start maybe, but at least he wouldn't accidentally mow over a cord.

"Hard to keep track," said Bob finally. "Got a few kids."

"Right. Well, I was thinking maybe Miles'd like to come over sometime. He could play with Matthew and Andy." She paused. Matthew wouldn't like it. He hated it when she tried to make plans for him. But the Fords were their neighbours and they barely spoke. She wasn't sure Matthew had ever even tried talking to Miles.

"Maybe I'll send him over," he said finally. "Might do him some good. Lazy little shit though." He looked her in the eye, as if daring her to disagree.

"Great. Just let me know beforehand, if you can."

Bob smiled, his teeth yellow and small. "Sixty-five if you throw in the mower," he said, licking his lips.

"Fine," she said. "When can you pick it up?"

"I'll bring over the truck tomorrow morning. That okay?"

She nodded. "And don't forget to ask Miles about coming over."

The man grunted again before turning his back on the garage and heading down the driveway.

MILES FORD

He stood outside the trailer shaking. The palm of his left hand bled into his pocket and he could feel it swelling where his dad had hit him again with the car antenna.

His dad was still yelling, his voice echoing inside the trailer, metallic and harsh. The Doberman sat alert beside the metal steps, its eyes fixed on him. He couldn't remember ever seeing the dog sleep. He took his hand out of his pocket and saw the beginnings of clotting, the blood drying slightly and the swelling turning purple. It was his fault. Trying to steal money while his father was napping. His father had opened his eyes and shouted at him to empty his pockets.

His hand throbbed.

He scanned the junkyard, breathing hard, his lungs crumpling like tinfoil and then expanding less each time as he fought back tears. The dog barked once as he walked down the potholed driveway, less junk and old tires with each step. He turned left towards the stop sign and walked along the telephone wires' looping shadows.

An empty A&W root beer can lay in the ditch and he retrieved it and stood it on end, crushing it with his foot and kicking it as he walked. Matthew and Josh would have passed it back and forth.

When he reached the stop sign he kicked the can into the ditch and picked up a rock and threw it, missing the sign. All at once he was self-conscious, and he looked around to see if anyone had seen his first throw.

No one.

He chose another stone, felt its smooth surface in his right hand. He threw it sidearm and the metal rang and shook with the impact. As the ringing faded he noticed the trickle of the river, and he climbed down from the road to the largest pool.

Shadows of tiny trout darted and shivered along the banks, their sides chrome-plated. He dipped his hand in the pool and felt the caked blood come loose and the throbbing cease for an instant in the quick cold. He rubbed the blood away and splashed his face as well, his cheeks stinging. He sat down, the throbbing pain returning as his hand warmed.

He could jump in, but his clothes would take hours to dry so late in the day, and he couldn't go in naked and risk someone seeing him. He climbed back up to the road instead and walked on the shaded side towards the pig farm. He stooped to pick up another stone, and as he did, crows scattered from the telephone wires. How'd birds get so smart? The butcher was pushing a wheelbarrow across the farm to a shed and he watched the man until he disappeared into the back of the deli.

Miles walked down the small drive leading to the front of the deli, paused, then stepped inside. He'd been there before with his dad ages ago, but never alone. Never without money.

The butcher had been scrubbing his hands and he looked up and smiled, raising his eyebrows.

"I don't have any money," said Miles, scratching his ear.

He watched the butcher's eyes follow his purple hand and he pocketed it quickly.

The butcher started to speak, stopped, then finally seemed to find the right words. "Are you hungry?"

THE BUTCHER

He watched Miles leave the deli clutching a fistful of pepperoni sticks. The boy seemed short for his age, with brown matted hair and dark circles under his eyes. Skinny and hard, like wire fencing. He'd never let his own son wander around covered in dirt and blood. But a lead ball of guilt in his stomach betrayed him, and a voice whispered: *Where is your son? He could be dead and you wouldn't even know.*

He leaned forward on the counter, his hands slipping on the smooth meat-wrapping paper. He didn't think of his son enough. But he'd be here soon. Safe. Although not everyone who lived here was safe. Miles wasn't. When he had handed the boy the sticks of pepperoni, Miles had stepped back, as if getting ready to duck and run. And his hand had looked bad. Not just a slap on the wrist but a wound that bled.

He didn't mind the boy begging for food. After all, he could have tried to steal something. The butcher had done it himself growing up. Bread or candy when no one was looking. There was something wrong with Miles though. His posturing was off, as though he'd given up. He didn't have any spark, not even enough to get into mischief, as if he was wandering through purgatory, a ghost on Deloume.

A breeze wafted into the deli, blowing the rich manure stink of the pig and dairy farms away from him and replacing it with scents of pine, dry grass and, for an instant, apples. He stepped through the back door and looked out over the farm, his vision blurring. He'd had a prescription filled for glasses but he hadn't picked them up yet. Secretly he was hoping he'd wake up one day with perfect vision, that maybe it was just allergies or the spices from the pepperoni bothering his eyes. He hated to think that he was getting old without his family, and he hated the idea of spending money on something he might not really need.

The pigs were in their covered trough, hiding from the sun's growing heat. Beside the deli the earth was damp around a leaking outdoor tap, and tiny drops of water shone on the grass like glass Christmas ornaments.

Laughter wavered through the air as a group of children rode past the farm on bikes, gliding down the road, the silver spokes of their tires spinning over the dusty gravel. He watched them pedal out of sight, so whole and alive, and then he thought of the other boy, his stooped shoulders and dirty clothes, the way he dragged his feet as he walked. Miles inhabited a different world, and he found himself struggling even to remember the boy's face.

The night before he'd left home he'd sat on the edge of his son's bed. His son had just stared at him, eyes wide. No signs of sleepiness. And he'd tried to think of what to tell the boy. But what could he say? How could he make a child understand that he was leaving to start something new and good for them, leaving so they could be happy together? Maria understood. She knew that there wasn't much for them there. That everything was so uncertain. They needed a place to live that offered them something, a place where they could hope for more than just hanging on. A future for their son. But Petr? How could he understand that?

Finally his son had spoken, catching him off guard as usual.

"What's Canada like, Father?"

It was the first time he'd realized he didn't have a clue. He'd spent so much time planning and thinking about how to get out of the country, how to start a new life, that he'd barely considered the place he'd end up. Canada. It sounded like a dream. And that was what he'd said to his son. That it was beautiful. That there was room for everyone. And plenty of work to go around.

"Won't you be lonely?" his son had asked.

"Only for a little while."

But that hadn't quite worked out. Not yet. And he'd had grander ideas about work too. Maria wouldn't be happy about the pig farm. He could almost hear her voice asking him why they'd travelled halfway around the world just to keep pigs. There were plenty of pigs back home too, she'd remind him. But there were other things here to be thankful for: a small grocery store and school in Mill Bay, just a short drive away. And colleges in cities not too far off. Maria could take classes if she wanted. Once they'd established themselves a little. Bought a car. And if they could save any money, who knew what might be possible?

One last question before his son had fallen asleep.

"Will I have friends there? When I come to Canada?"

"Of course," he'd said. "Of course."

And so he would. Maria couldn't argue with that. Not with all the families that lived nearby. And the children had such freedom. Riding bikes. Playing in the forest or down by the river. Everything seemed so ready for his family. So possible.

He thought again of Miles. Of how different he was. How alone.

A cobalt dragonfly zigzagged up and over the deli, and he squinted to watch it, then looked around him for another, his eyes coming to rest on a butterfly lying still at his feet, its white and black wings open. Water from the tap had fallen on it and tiny droplets magnified the patterns of white ovals on black.

He stood quietly and watched the dead butterfly for what seemed like hours, unable to look away.

SAM TOEWS

He reached down and patted the dog's head, combing its black and brown fur against the grain with his fingers. The dog lay at his feet panting, its tongue out tasting the air. One of its ears flopped.

"Who feeds you boy?" he asked. He leaned on the door frame of the farmhouse, the porch roof shading him from the sun. The dog looked up at him. "Maybe no one, eh?"

He walked inside and grabbed an old wooden bowl from the kitchen. He opened the fridge and took out a pot of leftover stew, spooning most of it into the bowl.

"Here ya go boy," he said, putting it on the floorboards of the porch.

He wondered who the mutt belonged to. Seemed like the thing had been coming around for ages now, always hungry. But there was no shortage of dogs around, that was sure. Never had been. Not even when he was a kid. Mongrel'd probably been here longer than most of the families. A hell of a lot longer than the butcher across the way. And the Chois—well, just the woman now. Even Al and Beth were relative newcomers, at least to the road. Fine by him though. Good to see new faces every now and then. Better than some of the old ones. Take the Fords. Never did like Bob much. Too severe. Always had been.

Even when Bob's dad used to drive the two of them around in that old TR6 when they were barely teenagers, he and Bob squished into the passenger seat, flying up and down Deloume in an orange blur. No dogs keeping up with them then.

"Not even you, boy," he said, patting the dog's side.

Yeah, new faces were a good thing. But he wasn't no newcomer, that was sure. His grandfather had cleared the land and he used to tell him stories about the early days. How some bushwhacked old surveyor had paid him and a few others in land titles for work clearing a logging trail. No rhyme or reason to it. Up and hanged himself on Mount Baldy, the old coot. Found him there days later. Named the road after him. Just them and a couple other families for miles then, his grandfather friendly with old man Ford, the two of them making money selling lumber as they cleared trees. Jesus, it must have taken years. Felling and hauling two-hundred-foot cedars and Doug-firs. Dynamiting stumps. Hard to believe the grass and clover his cows grazed over used to be forest.

The dog licked out the bowl and looked up at him.

"Oh no. That's it. You're not the only one who's hungry," he said, adjusting his baseball cap. Feeding time. He gave the dog one more pat and then shooed it off the porch, watching as it wandered down the driveway to Deloume.

JOSH

He watched Katie's hands as she pretended they were pistols. All wrong. No kickback. And the sounds wrong too. High-pitched. He never should have agreed to play with a girl, but Matthew had insisted on playing by himself again. Why the heck would anyone want to play alone?

Katie looked at him, flicking her brown ponytail over her shoulder. They stood on her front lawn, two houses down from his place and six up from Matthew's.

"Why aren't you shooting?" she asked.

"'Cause you're doing it wrong."

"Nuh uh, my cousin taught me. This is how cowboys shoot."

He groaned. She'd said he could have a cookie if he played with her but he was losing his appetite.

"Say the Indians have us surrounded," said Katie.

He sighed but didn't argue, instead lining up the sights on his imaginary rifle and making a proper sound as he picked off a brave.

"Say you get hit by an arrow," said Katie.

"What? Why me?"

"Because you're fat," she said. "You're a bigger target. And you keep bumping into me. You're a klutz."

He stared at the girl for a moment to see if she was joking.

She wasn't smiling. He fell over holding his side. At least he could lie down this way. He was tired and the whole thing was getting stupid. He lay flat on his back, hands over his chest, the fresh-cut grass pricking the back of his neck.

"No," said Katie. "You're not dead. You have to put one knee up. That means wounded."

"I know what it means."

"Hush," said Katie. "Don't make it worse."

He opened an eye and saw the girl leaning over him, her forehead wrinkled with concern. Still no sign of a cookie. But he didn't feel like going home yet. His parents were there, arguing about nothing as usual.

"Say I'm a nurse now and I have to take care of you," said Katie.

"Say I'm getting hungry."

"Say we fall in love and decide to get married."

He sat up. Katie knelt beside him, eyes closed, lips puckered. He stood and ran, not looking back until he'd reached Deloume.

ANDY

The girl walked towards him, a white veil over her face. He looked down at his hands. Pink Cracker Jack rings.

Two.

"Katie, you have to walk slower," said Elaine. "Otherwise people won't be able to see your dress properly."

Elaine stood beside him, holding a black book, dark hair falling out from under a round black hat.

Big hat.

A line of dolls sat on the lawn watching them. He wanted to put the rings in his mouth but he didn't. Instead he watched Katie's feet.

One. Two.

The grass bent beneath them.

When she reached him she stared at his eyes through the veil. He looked down at the rings again.

"Cookie," he said.

"Shhh," said Elaine. "The ceremony's started. You can't talk."

Be quiet.

"We are gathered here today—" said Elaine, pausing as a dog up the road barked, "to—"

"Skip to the kissing part," said Katie.

"Okay. Andy, do you take Katie to be your awful wedded wife?"

"Stop it!" cried Katie. "Do it right!"

Yelling in his ears. He covered them with his hands, letting the pink rings fall onto the lawn. He watched the two girls argue as they bent down to pick up the rings.

Angry.

He turned and ran down the driveway, hands over his ears, eyes on his shoes.

MATTHEW

The dusty shoebox was heavy and had no lid, and the worn cardboard tipped and twisted in his hands when he took it down from the shelf.

He put the box on the cold floor of the unfinished basement of their split-level and sat down. The room around him was all wood frame and cement, and it was filled with boxes of baby clothes and old toys. Things his mom knew Bob Ford wouldn't take away. He liked the feel of the cement floor, and he liked having a door nearby. An escape route. The house was built into a small hill, so only parts of the basement were underground, and there was a door off the side. He rummaged through the keys with his fingertips and felt the cold, oily dust of old steel and brass. He rubbed his fingers together then stirred the keys again. They didn't move easily in the box, their small teeth gripping a mess of positions, as if magnetic. The box smelled like his dad's collection of pennies. He'd remembered the box last night but hadn't had time alone to sort them yet. He wondered if any of them would fit the orange car's glove compartment. Probably not, but maybe he could jam one inside and get the old lock to turn.

The keys had come from all over, and he recognized some from lost bike locks, old mailboxes and miscellaneous padlocks.

But some of them looked older. All together there were at least twenty-five of them. Probably lots of them had been lost and then found again after they'd been replaced, but who threw away keys? Maybe some of them had even come with them from the Prairies—so long ago he couldn't even remember.

He heard the shuffling of feet and looked up. His brother stood in the doorway, his blue eyes fixed on the box.

"Cookie," said Andy, rubbing his hands on his sides as if trying to wipe off dirt or stretch his T-shirt into a more comfortable size. "Keys."

"Go away. I'm busy." He waved his brother away but Andy didn't move.

"Busy keys," said Andy, giggling.

Matthew cocked his head to the side and made eye contact with his brother. Andy looked away immediately, his eyes resting on his feet, which were stuffed into their dad's brown slippers. He slid his feet in and out.

"Go away Andy. I need to be alone."

Andy giggled again and disappeared from sight, his footsteps loud up the stairs to the kitchen. Matthew tipped the shoebox on its side, spilling the keys onto the concrete floor. He began arranging them into groups by size and colour. A glove compartment key would probably be small, but that wasn't always true, as sometimes the same key worked for a car's doors, ignition and glovebox. He'd tried out his dad's keys once, when his parents were over at the Henrys' having coffee. He hadn't driven the car, just opened all the doors and started it. The vibration of the engine had scared him a little, and he hadn't tried it again.

He was suspicious of the gold-coloured keys. Too many

stories about fools' gold. And things that were bright outside were usually poisonous. Snakes and spiders. Some berries. You had to be careful. And the lock on the glovebox had been silverish through the rust anyway.

He chose seven in the end that looked like they might work. It was a long shot, but if the lock was old enough he might just be able to get it to turn. He pocketed the keys he'd chosen and then began heaping the others back into the shoebox.

His brother appeared at the door again, this time skiing inside on the huge slippers.

"You back already?"

"Feet," said Andy, pointing and laughing.

He wondered how long he'd been sorting keys. He glanced at his plastic digital watch. Almost half an hour. But it had only felt like a few minutes.

"How come time doesn't always feel the same?" he asked Andy.

Andy stopped and looked at the keys on the floor and in the shoebox.

"I?" he said.

"Don't you ever wonder about that? Or is it always the same for you?"

Maybe it was always the same for everyone but him.

Andy sat down with his legs out in front, his feet cartoon-strip big. He never understood anything. It wasn't his fault though. But then, whose fault was it? His mom and dad's? Had they done something to Andy when he was inside their mom? Had there been an accident? His mom said sometimes these things just happened, and that God loved everyone anyway, but why was he normal and his brother not?

He left Andy stacking the keys in patterns and put on his shoes at the side door.

"Boys! Dinner's ready!"

His mom's voice was sharp, and he knew it wasn't a suggestion. Mealtimes weren't negotiable, even if he was trying to uncover a lost secret in the forest. He kicked off his shoes. He'd go later.

"Coming!" he shouted back.

"And find your brother!" his mom yelled.

He put his hand on Andy's shoulder, and his brother shrank away from his touch.

"Come on, time for dinner."

He was always helping out with Andy. He didn't really mind though. Somebody had to look out for him. Andy had stacked the keys in a vertical line between his legs.

"You have an extra leg," he said.

Special. Different. Retarded.

"Leg," said Andy, giggling.

Andy stood and ran up the stairs to the kitchen, one slipper on, stumbling over each step. Matthew picked up the other slipper and followed.

He washed the smell of the keys off his hands at the kitchen sink and marvelled that what he had felt on his skin after handling the metal had been invisible. See-through dirt.

He sat in silence across from his brother while they ate meat loaf, Kraft dinner and raw carrot sticks. Andy squirted too much ketchup on his macaroni and started to cry until their dad scooped most of it off with a spoon. His parents talked about the mess in the Fords' yard, and his mom kept saying the word "disaster." He tried to figure out what she meant. If it weren't for the Doberman he would spend all day exploring all the old stuff there. Miles was lucky.

His dad started complaining about how the neighbourhood dogs were going wild, chasing his car on the way to work. He imagined running after a car and grabbing onto the bumper. Would his legs just drag and get all cut up, or would they fly out behind him like Superman? Probably not a good idea to ask. His mom said she was worried about Irene Choi up the road because she was going to have a baby and it wouldn't have a dad. He'd only met Mr. Choi once but he'd seemed nice. He wondered what it was like getting shot. If you could feel the bullet going into you or if it was too fast.

"Any news about Al's boy?" asked his dad.

His mom shook her head. "No. Beth's pretty upset, of course. She says he's not taking it well."

"Dad, do you think they're ever gonna find Carson's plane?" he asked.

His dad looked at him and sighed. "I have no idea. A lot of bush pilots die on the job."

"David! They're still looking."

"I know, I'm just trying to be realistic. It's been more than twenty-four hours."

His parents started talking like he wasn't there again, and he wondered if there were any airplane parts in the Fords' lot. He'd only met Carson once or twice when he was younger, but he knew what he did. A real-life bush pilot.

"Matthew!" His dad's voice brought him back to the table. His parents were staring at him and he realized he'd missed a question.

"Look," said his mom, "I know you and Josh have been friends forever, but would it kill you to play with Miles sometime?"

He shrugged. No one told grown-ups who to spend time with.

"Let him be, Avril," said his dad, and they started arguing quietly.

He caught his brother grinning at him from across the table.

"Keys," said Andy under his breath.

He smiled back.

IRENE

She opened the top drawer of the dresser and took out the folded Canadian flag. She'd never unfolded it because she was scared it would never quite crease the same, like a map that refused to be put away. She pressed the flag to her face and breathed in, but it just smelled like the dresser, a mix of pine and clean laundry. She put it back next to the small black box that contained her husband's Medal of Bravery and shut the drawer, sitting on the end of the bed, her belly resting on her thighs. The bump of her belly button poked at her T-shirt.

Evening sunlight warmed the blue bedspread and she ran her hand over the fabric beside her. The phone rang but she didn't move to answer it. It would be her mother again. She was just doing her best. Her part. But the pressure to move back to Busan was building. She could hear it in her mother's tone, in the way she pronounced words as if the distance between them required her to push them out harder, force them across the Pacific. She wasn't rude exactly, but she made it clear that if Irene were home everything would be easier.

"Not for me," her mother had said. "For you."

The phone stopped ringing.

Home.

She imagined meeting her parents at the airport in Gimhae. Her mother would make a big show of it all, crying hysterically so that everyone would watch them. And her father would just stand there, sullen and distracted, paying more attention to the people watching than to her. He was the one who should understand it all best. After all, he'd been almost sixteen when the war finished. He'd lost a brother and close friends. Not that he'd talk about it. She'd tried before she'd left but it was like teaching a stone to speak. She'd asked question after question until finally he'd put his hand on her shoulder and smiled.

"Sue Hwa. How can you ask me to talk about things I want to forget, and things I hope you never see for yourself?"

She'd cried in her bedroom afterwards. Just knowing that he would never tell her, never help her understand him, had hurt worse than anything he could have said.

Her mother had been ten when the war finished. She didn't mind talking about it but she didn't seem to remember much. Just that there hadn't been enough food and that her mother and aunts had cried a lot. She talked more about how things were in the late fifties and sixties. About how their house was gone and entire cities rubble and dust. About how hard it was to go back to normal life without knowing who was where, and what had happened to so many people.

"That is what makes Korea such a special country," she'd told her. "We had to start again with nothing only a few years ago. And now look."

But she had looked, and it hadn't been enough to keep her there. All she'd seen was the same old Korea. The same expectations. The same family that just wanted her to marry a businessman and give birth to sons. The appearance of the country changed daily, new buildings and suburbs springing up as though they'd been planted and were sprouting at will. But some things, family, the suffocating cultural stigmas, stayed the same through it all.

She lay sideways on the bed and held her arm up over her head, the setting sun reflecting off the silver bracelet that hung loose. Joseph had given it to her. He'd given her the thing and the word.

Bracelet.

She didn't have the energy to cry.

For the thousandth time she tried to imagine how it had happened, putting together pieces from the official phone call, from the letter, from the TV. She saw Joseph walking on sand that turned to loose dirt and short pines, the desert slowly becoming wet and transforming into the lush hills around Busan, the two wars of her imagination melding.

A squad of soldiers moved from tree to tree, surrounding a cluster of tents, moving in and pointing their weapons at people huddled around a small fire. She tried to see Joseph among them in the desert along the Kuwaiti border, but again pines stretched up towards a paper-ash sky, her husband's face dark with paint, his rifle seemingly joined to his fingers, the oily metal an extension from bone.

A boy ran out from behind the huddled group carrying a rifle. Everyone started yelling and Joseph and the boy both hesitated, staring at each other. The boy was so thin, dirty arms and bare feet. She couldn't see his face. Joseph lowered his gun and put out his hand but one of the other soldiers stepped forward, startling the boy so he pulled the trigger, the gun spinning out of his hands as the soldiers opened fire on his small body. Joseph fell to his knees, his face a mask of war paint, the whites of his eyes disappearing as his blackened lids closed slowly and he toppled sideways.

AL HENRY

He could hear Beth putting away the dinner dishes in the kitchen, and the clack and clatter of plate on plate and the thud of cupboard doors became a familiar rhythm down the hall. They'd tried to talk about it but it hadn't gone well. They'd ended up just sitting across the table staring at one another. What was there to say? One of his paintings on the study wall was behind glass and he saw the outline of his reflection in it. He tried to fill in his own greying hair and the lines beneath his eyes, and as he re-created himself he saw a face, but it wasn't his own.

He rummaged through a drawer in his desk until he found the newspaper clipping with the photo. He studied it and put it down on the desk with a jar of white spirit holding it in place. He organized his easel and brushes and began to paint, slowly and carefully at first, then faster as he gained confidence, the smells of linseed and turpentine familiar and soothing, his own blend of incense. It'd been ages since he'd painted a portrait but he tried not to think about it, instead focusing on the task at hand, his thoughts ordering themselves, lining up in a way they only did when he was working. As the image took shape and came to life, he felt sweat bead on his forehead and run down his temple. The oils on the canvas looked right, and he thought about leaving it alone, letting the light layer dry. He massaged the dull ache of arthritis in his wrist. He heard the door open and knew that Beth was watching him.

"Do you recognize him?" he asked without looking up.

"My God," she said. "It's Joseph Choi."

He looked at the canvas and wondered what had possessed him to paint his dead neighbour. He'd seen the picture in the newspaper when it had happened two months back, Joseph's smile too wide, his crisp uniform impossibly well ironed, and it had reminded him of putting on his own uniform for the first time. Like new skin. Maybe that was why he'd kept the clipping. He hadn't known Joseph well. He and Irene had seemed to inhabit their own world, which was fair enough. They'd been newlyweds and they were still young. When he'd read Joseph's name in the paper the black ink had seemed so final, and the strangeness of the name had stood out. It was such an obviously Canadian construction, the Korean family name with the English Biblical name tacked on to the front. His own name seemed equally strange. Al Henry—a far cry from his given title in one of the island's Coast Salish dialects. Of course, he'd yet to find anyone off the reserve who could pronounce his Hul'q'umi'num' name. So it lay unused, as if mothballed and stored in the back of a closet, waiting.

He wondered what Joseph's real name had been. And Irene's?

It was easy to see why they all did it. Trying to make it easier for themselves or their children to fit in. He'd done the same for Carson. As if no one would notice the colour of their skin.

His mind wandered outside and up the road to Irene's house. He imagined her there alone, pregnant, receiving the phone call . . .

Beth had visited her right away, brought her groceries and done her best to look after her. But that was Beth's way, always willing to spend time helping other people. What had he done for Irene? Just avoided her. Every time he saw her all he could think about was that woman. Sheet-white face. Lying there in the cold. Forty years ago now.

Any idea what mul means?

Sure, that's easy. Means "water."

JOSH

I'm a robot.

He glided down Deloume Road, past Irene Choi's place, Matthew and Andy's driveway and the one-storey bungalow where the Henrys lived. As the road levelled out he forced his knees into motion and gritted his teeth, putting his full weight down on each pedal in turn, his legs heavy, sweat beading and cooling on his forehead as he gained speed down the small hill to the river. When he reached the stop sign he hammered back on the right pedal, letting the rear tire fishtail to a stop in the dust. He looked back and made a mental measurement of how long the skid mark was.

Not bad, but he'd done better.

He leaned his bike against the wooden pole of the stop sign and climbed down to the river. He had hoped to see Matthew's bike already leaning against the sign when he arrived. Maybe they weren't done eating dinner. Still, even playing alone was better than kissing Katie.

He was gasping for breath when he reached the pool, his lungs still on fire from the ride.

His insides weren't robotic.

It would be getting dark soon but he still had a little time before bed. He sat on the roots of a tree and waited for his breathing to level out. When he was younger he'd had asthma, but not any more. Now he could keep up with Matthew most of the time, and he was faster going downhill.

Because you're fat.

Matthew never made fun of him like Katie had. Stupid girl. Just because he was big. Matthew was never that bossy. His friend did always seem to know which direction to run or ride though. He couldn't remember a time when Matthew didn't know what to do. But he kinda liked that. Matthew wasn't mean about it, and it meant he didn't have to think when they were together. He could just play. Andy was lucky to have an older brother like him. He wondered what it would be like to have a brother. His parents wouldn't get angry at him as much, that was for sure. Matthew's parents spent all their energy worrying about Andy, and most of the time Matthew could do just about whatever he wanted. Sometimes he had to bring Andy with him though. The last time they'd tried to catch trout from the river Andy had come along, and he'd kept throwing sticks into the water and giggling and clapping his hands. Everyone knew you couldn't catch fish if you were too noisy.

He picked up a stone and tossed it into the pool, breaking the glossy surface. Ripples spread. He picked up another stone and threw it underhand in a high arc, listening for the gurgle-burp as the pool swallowed it.

He reached for another but paused. Tiny circles of reddish brown splattered the rocks beside him. Like paint, or dried blood from a nighttime nosebleed on his pillow. He stood and swivelled around to see if anyone was behind him. He was alone, the shadows around him growing. He checked the rocks to see if there was a mouse or newt stomach somewhere nearby, but there were only those few drops of blood, dark and dry over the powder white and green stones.

MILES FORD

He hid behind a tree as the truck passed, driving slowly. It was his dad out looking for him. If he found him he'd hit him again. Maybe worse. He waited until the truck was out of sight then cut through the forest until he came to Katie and Elaine's lawn.

The girls sat on the grass pouring imaginary tea for a circle of stuffed animals and dolls. He stood behind a tree at the edge of the property. It was getting dark. He'd never been this close to their house before, but he'd seen them play on the road and drive by in their parents' car. He'd finished eating his pepperoni sticks and his tongue still tingled from the spices. The girls were talking like grown-ups. Like the stuffed animals and dolls were children.

"No you can't have another cup silly, you haven't even finished your first," said Katie, frowning at a Barbie.

"The same goes for you," said Elaine, shaking her finger at a teddy bear whose head drooped down so that it looked ashamed.

What would happen if he left his hiding spot and stepped onto the lawn? They'd never asked him to play before, but maybe they'd just never had the chance. They didn't go to the same school as the other kids on the road. Their parents drove them to a private school an hour away. He'd heard Matthew talk about them down by the river. He said it was a stuck-up school. Girls only.

"This is boring," said Elaine. "Too bad you scared away the boys."

"It wasn't me, it was your fault. You didn't do the ceremony right," said Katie.

He stepped out from behind the tree. Katie saw him first and covered her mouth, gasping like she was on TV. Elaine turned around and stared at him. He walked over to them and stood with his hands at his sides, like he did when he first met a dog, careful to avoid eye contact and not make any sudden movement.

"What do *you* want?" said Katie.

He wasn't sure if it was really a question.

"Your name's Miles, right?" said Elaine.

Again it didn't really sound like a question, but the girls both looked at him like they wanted an answer, so he nodded.

"You live in a junkyard."

"Katie!" said Elaine.

"Well he does."

"But it's not nice."

"Are all of these dolls and things yours?" he asked.

"Of course," said Katie. "It's not like we stole them."

Elaine frowned at her sister. "Do you have a lot of toys and things?" she asked.

"No," he said. He couldn't think of anything else to say and he looked back over his shoulder at the trees lining the lawn.

"You smell funny," said Katie. "Like old shoes."

"Katie, be nice," said Elaine. "It's not his fault."

"It's gross."

He felt his face going red. It had been a mistake. They didn't want to talk to him.

"If you don't have any toys, what do you do all the time?" asked Elaine.

He thought about it. He couldn't tell them about his hiding place.

"He doesn't have any friends, I bet," said Katie.

"Katie, that's not true," said Elaine. "He probably has lots. Or some."

Both girls looked at him.

"I gotta go," he said.

Katie smirked, but Elaine leaned over to her sister and whispered something.

"Gross!" said Katie.

He felt like he was standing in front of two grown-ups. His parents maybe. Like they could see right through his head and read his brain. His secrets.

"I dare you," said Elaine.

"That's not fair," said Katie.

"You're chicken."

"Nuh uh, it's just gross."

He took a step backwards, but Elaine stood up and grabbed his hand. He stood as still as he could, afraid to breathe, his chest tight.

"Katie wants to kiss you," said Elaine.

He swallowed and looked at Katie. He didn't think she did. She acted like she hated him.

"You promise not to tell anyone?" asked Katie.

Elaine nodded.

"You too?" The girl looked at him.

Who would he tell? He nodded.

"Cross your hearts," said Katie.

Elaine crossed her heart with her finger and he did the same.

"Hope to die."

Elaine nodded. He copied her.

"Stick a needle in your eye."

Elaine closed her eye and touched the lid. He copied her again and his eye started to water. Spices from the pepperoni. He tried to blink away the burning but it wouldn't stop. He watched the girls with one eye closed.

Katie stood up and shut her eyes. She leaned forward and puckered her lips, pressing them so hard together that they wrinkled and turned white. Elaine pushed him towards the girl who hated him but wanted to kiss him. He'd never kissed a girl before. Hadn't really ever wanted to. His eye burned and a tear ran down his cheek. If he kissed her maybe they'd want to play with him again. Maybe they wouldn't hate him.

He leaned forward and pressed his lips onto hers. She smelled like soap and her lips were surprisingly hard. The kiss barely lasted a second before Katie opened her eyes and jumped backwards.

"Eww!" she yelled. "He smells like a garbage can!"

"Katie! You're so mean!" said Elaine. "Look, you made him cry."

He wiped tears from his watering eye. "No," he said, but Katie cut him off.

"He smells and he's a crybaby!"

She grabbed Elaine's hand and the two girls ran giggling across the lawn into the house, leaving him standing alone in the fading light, surrounded by a circle of dolls and stuffed animals.

BETH

She tried to smile at Irene as she closed the fridge. Irene was gorgeous but she clearly hadn't slept. Dark rings puffed out beneath her eyes. Her black hair had been hastily pulled back and several strands fell over her forehead and temples. Still, her high cheekbones and smooth skin made her look even younger than twenty-five. And she was tiny—she'd barely put on enough weight.

"Is there anything else I can bring you?"

Irene shook her head. She was still too shy to accept much help, but that was fine. She was getting over it. The embarrassment of needing help at least.

"Thank you," said Irene, for the third time in five minutes.

"You don't have to keep saying that Irene."

The girl blushed and pointed to the living room. Beth sat in the rocking chair and Irene lowered herself onto a cushion on the floor, her belly resting on her lap. It was hard to imagine the floor being more comfortable than a chair, but maybe it was just a matter of what you were used to.

"Oh, I forgot. Tea," said Irene. "Do you want tea?"

Beth smiled. "No, I'm fine thanks." She'd tried Korean green and jasmine teas with Irene before. Terrible flavours, especially the green. So bitter and grassy-tasting. And it was too late in the day for caffeine. Nice of her to offer though. She could sense Irene relaxing a bit. Words seemed to come more easily to her when she didn't feel self-conscious.

"How are you sleeping?"

Irene shook her head. "I can't," she said. "Sometimes."

It wasn't uncommon. To be expected really. Never mind losing her husband—the pregnancy was enough. Once, before she'd retired from the maternity ward at Vancouver General, Beth had met a woman whose husband had left her when she was eight months along. The woman had said he hadn't liked the changes to her body. As simple and pathetic as that. She recalled the way the woman had sounded, her matter-of-factness when she said she often woke at night and felt someone next to her, but that when she reached out there was no one there. A ghost sleeping beside her. Finally the woman's sister had come to stay with her for the last two weeks of her pregnancy. At least that woman had had family to support her. A sister and a brother-in-law. Irene had no one. Eight months along.

She and Al had skipped all of that. Or missed it. She'd been past it when they'd met. She'd had relationships when she was younger of course, but nothing serious enough for her to consider having a child. Anyway, Al had Carson from his first marriage. Carson.

"You are upset?" asked Irene.

She was caught off guard. She hadn't told Irene about the plane yet. Was she that transparent? She grasped the armrests of the rocking chair and took a deep breath before telling her what had happened.

"I'm sorry," said Irene, and Beth could tell she was struggling to find words, that she wanted to say more but couldn't.

They sat in silence for a moment until Irene leaned over and touched her hand, then gasped and pointed to her belly.

"Feel," she said.

She put her hand on Irene's stomach as the baby kicked, and she laughed despite herself, Irene joining in, the sound filling the room like lights coming on after a power failure.

MATTHEW

He walked to the end of the driveway, Andy up ahead of him. Bob Ford's black truck rolled to a stop beside Andy, and Matthew walked faster towards the headlights that shone palely through the growing dark, as if under water.

"I asked you a question boy," said Bob out the window. Andy stood staring at one of the truck's tires.

Matthew stepped in front of Andy and looked at the outline of Bob's darkened face, letting his imagination fill in his small eyes and yellow teeth. The man's arm hung out the window, his thick wrist covered with dark hair, his knuckles rapping on the door as though keeping time, counting down to something.

"If you were my boy you'd show a little respect," said Bob to Andy.

"But he isn't," said Matthew, staring into the truck. "He doesn't wanna talk to you."

He felt his dinner churning, his stomach going watery, but he kept his eyes on the man.

"Your folks know you're out here?" asked Bob.

Matthew nodded.

"Yeah, well I sure as hell hope so." Bob leaned out the window and spat. "You seen my boy around?"

Matthew shrugged.

"You not talking either now? Something wrong with you boys?"

"I haven't seen him."

"You sure about that now?" asked Bob. "'Cause I'd hate to think you were hiding him from me."

"I'm sure," he answered, as he grabbed Andy's arm and pulled him back up the driveway.

"Sleep tight boys," said Bob after them. "And don't you let me find out you're lying to me neither."

April, 1899

The Douglas fir smouldered through the night and into the morning, sending up smoke signals and filling the air with the smell of charred pine needles. A parade of insects had evacuated the tree after the lightning strike, and he'd seen electrocuted moths drop from branches by the dozen, falling slowly, their wings glowing.

He held a Black Witch out in front of him, brown and grey with a hint of purple at the tail, its wingspan covering his palm. *Ascalapha odorata.*

Already named.

Gabriel's voice in the trees. Whispers. Forgotten names. Names that men like Cook, Vancouver and Douglas were oblivious to. He'd heard stories of the island's Natives and their languages, of how they often named things after their behaviour or appearance. *Ascalapha odorata.* The Latin so far removed from the thing itself. Like his own names: French, even though his mother insisted they were English through and through. His names weren't him. Or were they? Did he become his names, or did his names make him?

He stared up at the fir. Although it was more like a pine really—the tree had been poorly named. Even he could see that its cones didn't stand upright like a true fir's. In any case, it wouldn't be fit for lumber now. Too dangerous to take down.

A burning bush. A sign.

And no Douglas there to see it. They'd found him dead in Hawaii, caught in a wild bull trap. Cook had died in Hawaii too. Some paradise.

The promised land.

He took out his notebook and sketched the smoking tree, then turned the page and focused on a blackened seed cone. The memory of the lightning bolt crashed through his mind. He was the only man on earth to have seen it happen and now it was gone. He wished he could have caught the lightning somehow, pinned it to a piece of paper, his name forever tied to fire from the sky.

The Douglas Fir

The lightning-singed Douglas fir stands between Deloume Road and the dairy farm like a war-bombed church spire. Even though the top is charred and dead, the tree is still two hundred feet tall, and twisted bare branches jut from the thick, layered bark, one of them housing a bald eagles' nest. The branches on the bottom half of the tree are still growing, thick and full with flat evergreen needles and brown cones, the lowest branch twenty feet off the ground. White moths rest on the bottom branches, steal sugar and wait for the cool of summer dusk, when they drop like newspaper ash to flutter around the hulking tree trunk, their white wings catching the sun's tired light against a backdrop of bark and green.

I reach out and touch the tree. It's rough and pipe-smoke grey with age. Any signs of rich red and brown have faded, and the bark looks petrified. It covers the trunk in overlapping layers. I want you to say something, tell me what you remember, what you felt, but you just stand beside me looking up, as if it had never happened. As if nothing had changed.

"I don't belong here any more," I say, letting my hand fall from the tree. My gut twists and I feel that same guilt. That same panic. I breathe deeply, focus on the stunted crabapple trees growing in a ring around the giant, their humble branches bowing before the great trunk, their lichen-stained bark crumbling in the heat. And around the apple trees and along the farm's fence blue spruce grow in clumps, their needles dust-coloured. Above, a bald eagle circles then lands near the distant top of the scorched Douglas fir. The tree's high, needle-bare branches are the perfect lookout. I spot another bird, higher, wheeling on a current. They circle on convections from the hot earth, higher and higher without more than a tilt of their wings, until they become specks, scratches on the surface of the eye. And their wheeling air-current pattern mimics the concentric circles of trees and plants spreading out from the lookout—or is it the other way around?

I keep looking up at the sky but I can tell you're staring at me by the way my skin prickles.

I tell you that when I threw a rock through the hole in the stop sign for the last time, decades ago now, I wished to go back in time.

"Before it happened," I whisper. "To change things."

Your eyes wide, unmoving. Mouth open.

One of the eagles lands high on a charred branch. I wait for it to move but it stays perfectly still, a gargoyle looking down, and us tiny among the tangles of vines and underbrush.

ANDY

He held his mom's hand and watched the brown and black dog chase a car out of sight. Red car. Floppy ear. His mom tugged gently at his arm and they walked side by side up the road. He watched their feet.

One. Two.

They stopped and his mother's voice vibrated through the air. He looked up at a short woman with black hair. Her stomach fat. His mother put her hand on the woman's round tummy and smiled.

"Andy," she said. "Irene's going to have a baby."

Their voices hummed and he watched the woman's sandalled feet, then looked at his mother's. His mother's feet were bigger.

Two. Big. Two.

They were looking at him. He could feel their eyes on his hair, his forehead, his neck and shoulders. He waited for a moment listening, watching their mouths, trying to figure out why they were staring at him. Irene smiled and took his free hand, pressing it against her belly.

The baby kicked and his fingers tingled. He jerked back his hand and clenched his fist, holding it against his chest. Both women laughed as he started running. Fast. Away. His hand still full of electricity.

JOSH

He sat on his bike at the top of his driveway. It wasn't as long as Matthew's but it was steep, and he had to listen carefully to make sure that no cars were coming along Deloume before he pushed off, otherwise he'd have to stop at the bottom and lose speed.

A hummingbird hovered beside him and he stared at it. Matthew would know what kind of hummingbird it was probably, and how fast its wings moved, but he was playing alone again. He wished his friend hated playing by himself as much as he did. Maybe he'd stop by Matthew's place later to see if he was done being by himself.

A few days back they'd climbed as high as they could up a tree beside his house, Matthew on the opposite side of the trunk, the two of them so high the tree swayed when they leaned.

"Can you believe God actually made this tree?" he'd said.

"He's better at drawing than Mr. Henry," said Matthew.

"Do you think Spiderman will be in heaven?"

"Of course."

He wondered if Mr. Henry's son was dead. And if his parents already knew but hadn't wanted to tell him. He glanced at his bike tires and leaned forward to push on the front tread. It compressed a little. Should he fill up the tire with the basketball pump or leave it until later? The hummingbird was gone and he shivered despite the heat of the afternoon as Matthew's words tumbled through his brain.

"Do you ever wonder if maybe there is no God?" Matthew's voice had been hushed.

But he hadn't known how to answer, so instead of saying anything he'd just clung tightly to the tree, as though he were waiting for a strong wind to pass.

A fly circled and landed on his head, its drone stopping as it landed, as if it had swallowed its own sound. He didn't brush it away. There was no breeze. Branches and leaves hung hot and limp. He pushed off and let his weight roll the bike down the driveway.

ANDY

He walked home with his hand out in front of him, afraid to touch anything else in case he forgot the feeling. He watched his feet march up the driveway to his house and around back. He sat on the lawn. Bugs crawling through green.

Baby.

A hot tear ran down his cheek and gathered under his jaw. He looked at his hand. No cuts. No blood. He remembered picking blackberries and counting them as he placed them into an ice cream pail with a shoelace for a handle, his fingers stained.

His outstretched hand was clean, but he stared at it to make sure, then pressed it against the soft ground.

JOSH

He zigzagged down the road, waving at Irene and at Matthew's mom, and yelling at Andy, who was walking towards his own driveway holding one hand out in front of him. Andy didn't turn his head so Josh kept pedalling. He steered into a pothole that was too deep, his arms jarring on the handlebars. But his tires made it through and he kept riding.

A white truck was parked beside the stop sign and he skidded to a halt beside it. The driver sat with the window down, staring at a clipboard. The writing on the door of the truck said *Municipality of Mill Bay*. Josh sat on his bike and watched as the man got out and grabbed a tool box from the back of the truck. The man was tall and thin, and he wore blue jeans and a light blue collared shirt. He walked to the stop sign and unfastened the red octagon, struggling with each bolt, then carried it to the truck and threw it in the back.

Josh didn't like the look of things, the way the man's shirt was tucked into his pants with no belt, and him taking away the sign that he'd thrown so many stones at and through. The man was taking away part of his home, a lucky part too.

The man replaced the old sign with a new one that shone bright and smooth in the sun. He wondered if the man noticed that it was facing the wrong way, but he wasn't about to tell him.

At least it would look the same as the old one. When the man was finished he got back in his truck, checked something on his clipboard and drove off without even looking at him.

Josh spat through the dust cloud the truck threw up in his direction, then hopped off his bike and picked up a rock. He eyed the new sign carefully, cocked his arm and paused. He spat again and dropped the rock.

There was no hole to aim for.

AL HENRY

He gripped the handgun tight, squinted down the barrel and squeezed the trigger, watching holes open up on the target across his backyard. He lowered the gun and slipped on the safety, then pulled out his earplugs. The shock of the kick-back throbbed up and down his forearms. He breathed the faint, acrid smell of hot metal and gunpowder.

They'd yelled for him to stop, rifles raised to chest height. After a day of marching through the snow he'd almost just ignored them and kept walking, eager to get to the mess tent and find something warm to eat.

"Yeah you! You speak English?"

He nodded. "Yeah."

"Forget it Jerry, it's Al," said a soldier next to him. "He's not Korean."

The perimeter sentries eyed him then looked at each other, lowering their weapons.

"What is he then?" asked one of them.

The soldier next to Al laughed and slapped him on the back. "Why he's our very own redskin sharpshooter, ain't that right?"

Al grimaced and nodded, then brushed the men aside, trudging over the foot-packed snow towards a ring of green tents. One of the guards' voices carried over the wind in his ears.

"Sure as hell looks like a gook."

When he pulled out the earplugs the first thing he noticed was the silence around him. No dogs. No birds. Then slowly the subtle noises of insects, and a bark in the distance. He'd been painting all morning and into the afternoon, trying to perfect the portrait he'd started the day before. The first layers were pretty well dry already. It was always quicker in the summer.

But his concentration had started to slip, and he was too tense and worried to enjoy working. So he'd found his old pistol and set up a target. It was the first time he'd fired the gun for ages. He'd kept it oiled though. Old habit.

Out of the corner of his eye he saw Andy standing next to the house, pulling at his shirt as if he were nervous or uncomfortable.

"Are you looking for something?" asked Al, glancing around for a stray Frisbee or ball.

The boy shook his head.

"Then what do you want?"

"Loud," said the boy, his gaze shifting from the target to the gun in Al's hand.

"Yeah, well, it's a free country, right?" The boy wasn't in any hurry to disappear. "Are you gonna just stand there?"

Andy stepped forward, first one foot slowly, then the other, then three steps quickly until he was standing beside him.

"You shouldn't sneak up on me when I'm shooting." He spoke evenly, making sure to pronounce each word slowly.

The boy stretched out his hand, his eyes fixed on the gun.

"I don't think that's such a good idea, do you?"

"Be careful," said the boy abruptly, like he'd just remembered a word or a name he'd forgotten and had been searching for.

Al nodded and checked again that the safety was on. "Will you go home if I let you touch it? You can't hold it though, your mom'll probably want my hide just for letting you do this."

He waved Andy closer, the boy's eyes never leaving the gun. He held the pistol firmly as Andy reached out to touch it, his fingers shaking in the air an inch from it, as though the black metal were alive, a coiled snake.

"Hey Andy!"

Al turned and saw Matthew and Josh standing on the driveway, waving at Andy to come and join them. Andy seemed to hesitate so the two boys walked over.

"Sorry Mr. Henry, is he bugging you?" asked Matthew.

Al shook his head. "No, I think the sound of the gun just scared him a little, then maybe made him curious."

"Wow, a gun. Can we shoot it?" asked Josh.

"Do you have any idea what your mothers would do to me?"

Josh shrugged. The boy hadn't been expecting him to say yes.

"How are you boys today?"

"Terrible," said Josh.

Matthew nodded.

"But it's gorgeous out, and you're not in school."

"He took the old stop sign," said Matthew. "Josh saw him do it."

"Who did?"

"Some stupid guy," said Josh. "And he put up a new one."

"Does it still face the wrong way?" asked Al. He glanced at Andy and saw that his eyes still hadn't left the gun.

"Yeah. But the old one had a hole through the O," said Josh.

Al raised his eyebrows.

"If you throw a rock through it you get to make a wish," said Matthew.

"Well, that is too bad then," said Al, watching as Matthew grabbed his brother's hand.

"Is your son still lost, Mr. Henry?" asked Josh.

Matthew elbowed Josh in the ribs and the boy mumbled an apology, but Al forced a smile.

"It's okay. But yeah. He's still lost."

"Sorry," said Matthew.

"Yeah, sorry," added Josh.

Al watched them turn on their heels and head down the driveway, Matthew holding Andy's hand and Andy looking over his shoulder, craning his neck for one last glimpse of the gun.

IRENE

She hung up the phone but let her hand rest on the receiver, the moulded eggshell plastic warm against her fingers and palm. She sat on the floor, the curling phone cord over her feet.

Her mother wanted her home, but more than that, she wanted Irene to want to come home.

"There are many good men looking for young women here now," her mother had told her. "There aren't enough wives for all the men."

Wives? Or women? After all these years of prizing their sons, it had caught up with them. Maybe they should check the orphanages. So many girls. The thought surprised her. Was it bitterness? Yes, the emotion even tasted sour.

Not long ago her mother's words would have been encouraging and she might have felt some flicker of hope, but she was different now. It wasn't something she could undo, all the time away, all the things she'd seen.

Her brother had never even left Korea. He was only twenty, but still. Five years younger than her. The prince. That was how it felt. She'd been old enough to remember his arrival. Everyone in the family had called to congratulate her mother and father. Mostly her father. After all, what did women have to do with it? There was a saying in Korea that she'd learned then: *A daughter is a miss.* As though she'd been stillborn or miscarried. What did that make her brother? A prince. She'd even heard people asking her parents about their first-born. How was he? Was he strong and healthy? She wondered if anyone had called her parents after she'd been born.

A miss.

Her brother was spoiled rotten, too. When he'd left for military service their mother had wept, made a scene at the train station. She'd also cried when Irene had left for Canada, but nothing like that. People at the station had asked Irene if there'd been a death in the family. She'd almost wished it. Then there was her father. Telling her brother that when he came back he'd be the man of the house. Never mind that she'd trained as a teacher, started her first job in Busan. Never mind that every male had to complete twenty-five months of military service. They acted like he was a hero, when all he was doing was obeying the law. Students and professors at her university had lobbied for a reduced military service, and she'd marched with them. Korea needed to move into the twenty-first century, not glorify its military. It was different in Canada. At least men had a choice. Service in Korea wasn't heroism, it was a waste of time. Especially with the Americans still on the peninsula.

Was it possible that home was no longer home?

But she was still a foreigner here, and she missed her mother despite herself. Her in-laws lived in Toronto and they'd offered to let her stay with them until the baby was born, but they were total strangers, and so far away. They meant well, but in some ways they were even more traditional than her family back home, clinging to their patriarchal Confucian hierarchies as though those were what made them Korean. Her father-in-law had said they'd raise her son if she couldn't. If she needed help. She'd asked him if the offer would stand if she gave birth to a daughter, and just the way he'd hesitated had given him away. They hadn't spoken since.

She stood, her knees, hips then lower back popping in succession, and walked to the opposite wall of the living room, where she had thumbtacked photos of her family. She put her finger on the bottom of her mother's picture to hold it flat. She had her mother's inky eyes and broad forehead, but her cheekbones weren't as wide. Her mother's lips were thin and drawn, as if too much pursing and scolding had forced them inwards. She touched her own lips, felt their contours, the roughness of dry skin and the teardrop centre of her top lip. Over eight months since they'd said goodbye in Korea. When she let her mind wander she could almost smell her mother's apple shampoo mixed with the abandoned-closet smell of mothballs. She blinked back a tear, her eyes refocusing on the photo. Her mother had dyed her hair for it.

"Brown, like a Western woman. To show your new friends and family," she'd said.

Oma, I have no one to show this picture to. No one who understands.

But how could she ever go back? People would never look at her the same. She'd see it in their eyes. She'd know. There was no shortage of labels for women who married foreigners. She could hear the Ajumas whispering in the markets, the fish-stall vindictiveness of people who didn't even know why they cared.

Her mother had always been proud of her though, and had even encouraged her to take a chance on the foreigner. "He's Korean anyway," she'd said. "Even if he can't speak it well."

She wondered what her mother might have said if he'd been Caucasian or African. She smiled. She knew.

She lowered her hand to her belly.

So warm.

She rubbed the taut skin through her cotton shirt. Her mother had mailed the T-shirt to her. "Cheaper maternity clothes here," her mother had said, and Irene hadn't argued even though it wasn't true.

She leaned forward and kissed the photo.

Oma, I am your daughter and not your daughter. And there is no word for this in any language.

JOSH

He walked Matthew and Andy home, feeling the heat off the road on his bare ankles and shins.

"You didn't really tell Bob Ford off, did you?" he asked. Matthew nodded. "Were you scared?"

"A little," said Matthew. "But he was getting mad at Andy for nothing."

"But what if he'd got out of his truck?"

"I wish I had a gun like Al," said Matthew. "That'd show him."

He stopped and stared at Matthew but his friend didn't notice and continued walking, his eyes on Andy. Josh ran a few steps to catch up.

"You'd never shoot anybody though," he said.

"Yeah I would," said Matthew, kicking a rock into the ditch. "Naw, not for real. But maybe if they tried to hurt Andy."

"But you'd go to jail.".

"Yeah, but they wouldn't hurt Andy."

THE BUTCHER

He stood outside the small concrete slaughterhouse. His hands shook.

It didn't take a violent person to be a butcher. He wasn't. There wasn't any rage in him when he killed a pig. Really, killing a big animal was more of a science. A bolt right through the temple made the work go quickly and easily, but a mistake meant hours of hell to pay.

The sow had screamed. Not squealed or grunted. The damned thing had screamed. He'd mistimed it, made a huge mess of it, cracking the pig's skull but leaving it alive and thrashing. Blood everywhere. He'd been distracted. Thinking about his son again, letting his mind wander home instead of paying attention to the task at hand. He should have known better. It'd taken him all morning to clean up. It didn't happen often now, but when it did . . . He took a deep breath, watching his right hand tremble as he held it out, examining the thin two-inch scar that ran down the back of it from his knuckle.

It had happened the first time he'd butchered a pig. He'd been ten, about the age of some of the boys here, he guessed. Too young perhaps, but then things were different back home. And there hadn't been any laws about attending school. He remembered trying to slice open the pig's throat. He hadn't cut deep enough. Simple as that. He'd been overly tentative and indecisive, like a child trying to saw a wooden plank for the first time. His father had tried to hold the massive sow steady, but the adrenalin rushing through its two-hundred-pound body had been too much. The pig should have been restrained properly, tied tighter, but working in the slaughterhouse meant payment for quantity not quality, and rules were only rules when you got caught. The knots on the rope binding the sow's front legs had come undone and it had lurched up and thrashed its thick head sideways, knocking his hand into a nail jutting out from a board of the pen. He'd pulled his hand back in shock, tearing the skin and scraping bone on the rusted metal spike.

He touched the scar, thin now. At the time it had looked like he might lose his hand. The infection had caused a fever, and his father had worked overtime for months to pay for the penicillin. He had sworn to him he'd never have to work in a slaughterhouse again. But here he was. The farm and deli weren't anything like what he'd known as a boy though—the bloodstained walls and the stench of workers' sweat mingling with pig shit and the iron musk of blood.

He stared out over the patches of weeds that grew in almost daily among the snout and hoof craters, the yellow earth dry now, waiting for autumn rains to turn it brown. His hand had stopped shaking and he took a deep breath and exhaled slowly. He wondered if Miles would come by again. He felt nervous about interfering in anyone else's business—after all, he was still a newcomer—but how could those people treat their son like that? If his boy were here he'd live like a prince. Bacon and eggs every morning before school. Of course it was summer now, but he would find something for him to do. A trip perhaps, or sports. None of this wandering around alone. And his boy would have a comfortable bed in a cottage. Not just a corner in some rusting trailer. It must be like living in a tin can. The pigs had almost as much space.

He could go to the police about it. But then, if the boy's parents wanted to, they could make life very difficult for him. Foreigners with big mouths didn't last long. It was the same in his hometown. And he'd seen enough of the Fords to know that they wouldn't back down from a fight. They'd come into the shop once or twice and scowled at his prices—he'd been surprised by their oily skin and dirty clothes, by their apparent poverty, even in a place as lovely and full of opportunity as this. And he'd felt it even then. Fear. He was afraid of them. Afraid they'd try to push him out, or that they'd resent him for settling there, for not having to live in a trailer like they did.

But surely doing nothing was wrong too. A sin even. He eyed the shed where he kept his wheelbarrow and shovel. Perhaps he could clear some space? If he took off the lock and threw in a blanket, maybe Miles could sleep there. He wouldn't need more than a thin sheet for another few weeks yet. If the boy was sleeping at home, then fine, but if he was outside at night, at least he would have the option of shelter, however humble.

He walked to the small shed beside the deli and unlocked the door. It wasn't much space but once he'd taken out the wheelbarrow, shovel and spade there was room on the floor.

After sweeping the boards, he threw down some empty potato sacks and dropped a folded wool blanket on top of them. The shed was made of cedar planks and its wooden floor was elevated on six-inch stilts to keep it dry. The aging cedar boards still smelled sweet, like carrots, even as the outsides of the planks were weathering grey and beginning to splinter.

He left the door open.

BETH

She stared at the face of the dead man and felt the pace of her heart quicken. The dark brown eyes were disarming. Intense. She found herself waiting for them to blink.

They stood side by side, Al looking at the painting, his eyes bloodshot and his chin covered in grey stubble.

"What will you do with it?" she asked.

Al hesitated, then picked it up and carried it out of the room, starting down the stairs to the basement. He stopped and returned.

"Hell if I know," he said. "I don't even know why I painted it."

But Beth had a pretty good idea. He hadn't exactly avoided them, but she'd seen how relieved he was when Irene and Joseph had turned down invitations. It all had to do with Korea and Joseph and now his own son going missing. Was he trying to make up for something? Trying to deal with his memories of the war? Or was he just relating to Irene without meaning to?

"Irene—" she started, pausing as he made eye contact with her. She raised her eyebrows.

He sighed and nodded, then put on his shoes and left carrying the painting. She watched him from the kitchen window as he bent to pat the head of the brown and black dog that had been lying outside their front door all afternoon in the shade of the house. She couldn't figure out why he bothered to feed it. Surely its owner must take care of it. It was a little mangy, but that could just be age. It looked well fed. She tried to remember whom it belonged to. Avril and David? Sam?

What a day. Still no word about Carson's plane. The waiting was torture for Al. For them both. She'd only ever spoken with Carson a few times alone, once over the phone and he'd dropped by twice in the past year or so. He hadn't really shown any interest in her, which was what she'd expected. She didn't want to compete with his mother anyway. Of course he could have made a little more effort for Al's sake.

He didn't look like Al at all. Al could almost pass for white during the winter. Well, maybe that wasn't completely true, but Carson had such dark skin and he wore his hair long. And where Al's face was lean, his son's was square, with a thick jaw and broad forehead. Like his mother, she guessed.

She went down the short hallway to her husband's studio and flicked on the light. If Carson was dead, would Al keep all the paintings of airplanes lining the walls, or would they be too painful to look at? The room seemed to close in around her. She turned off the light and returned to the kitchen. She wasn't sure how she felt about the portrait of Joseph. Surely it had something to do with his nerves. His nightmares of Korea. Anxiety. All this waiting without knowing. What other explanation was there? Her hunch was that it would make Irene happy, but she couldn't quite find the words to ask him where exactly it had come from or what it meant. In some ways she was glad to see him taking a break from airplanes. They'd always impressed her and bothered her in equal measure. Beautiful really—their accuracy and the way he was able to catch light reflecting off metal.

But then also sad, or, no, that wasn't right. Not sad, just frustrated, or incomplete. It was hard not to feel that it was wrong to paint airplanes, to capture their image in a static medium. They were made to fly. Wasn't that what was so wonderful about them to begin with? His paintings were like butterflies on pins.

She took out a knife and a bag of Granny Smith apples for a crumble, skinning them and hollowing out the cores, then slicing. She'd been craving something sweet and warm in the evenings, and eating dessert out on the porch with a cool summer breeze tickling her ankles sounded right. She'd bake it now and eat it with Al. Take their time over it tonight. Al spent so much time painting nowadays. It didn't make her angry, or even resentful exactly, but retirement wasn't really all that it was cracked up to be. They'd both agreed that moving somewhere quieter was a good idea, but she was starting to have her doubts. At least when they'd lived in Vancouver there were more people around, her friends from the hospital. Maybe if they'd saved some money they could have travelled more, but their pensions wouldn't stretch very far. And now she couldn't quite figure out what she was supposed to do with her time. When she was younger she'd written poems and short stories, but the thought of picking up a pen and actually starting something seemed a bit ridiculous.

Al would be arriving at Irene's by now. How would it all go? He probably wouldn't tell her much about it. She could imagine him leaving the painting on Irene's doorstep. He had damn well better not. The last thing the poor girl needed was a painting of her dead husband appearing on her doorstep without explanation. She was stressed and exhausted enough. But Al had never been any good at expressing his emotions. Let alone to someone he barely knew. Maybe it all came out in the paintings. In the care he took with each stroke. When they'd first met he'd bought her flowers and chocolates but never given them to her. Some first date. She'd found them, with a card, in a Dumpster beside her apartment. She'd been taking out her garbage the next day and there they were. Just lying on top. But something about finding the dozen crimson roses in the trash had endeared him to her. Funny, he'd got over his shyness with her and done countless wonderful things, but if she hadn't seen those flowers she wouldn't have stuck it out at the start.

She put down the knife and dumped the apple slices into an oval baking dish.

He'd never painted her portrait. She'd often thought it would be romantic to pose for him. Nude. Even if she was a little past it. But she'd never asked. Not once. They'd been together for ten years and she'd never even brought it up. And now here he was painting his dead neighbour.

She turned on the oven then opened the window wider. Too hot to bake really, but it'd be worth it later.

Carson. She both wanted news and didn't. As long as that phone didn't ring they were still searching. The boy had a great reputation as a pilot. She couldn't figure out why he didn't work for a commercial airline. More money, less risk. But maybe it was the risk that did it. Maybe he liked it. No wonder Al was proud of him.

She opened a bag of brown sugar and the scent of blackstrap molasses filled the kitchen.

AL HENRY

He walked down his driveway and turned onto Deloume. He probably should have called Irene first but he didn't want to procrastinate. And he could always just leave the painting on her doorstep if his courage failed. It was only a five-minute walk up the road.

He sidestepped a pothole and felt the prickle of the afternoon sun on the side of his neck and face. He glanced up at clouds that were turning the first shades of blue before purple. The trees lining the road would cast long shadows soon through the soft light, and there would be a bustle of movement as insects and birds prepared for the end of the day, those final stretches of wings and limbs before the night watch took over.

He wondered how Irene would react to the gift. If he could even call it that. Guilt crept into his temples in a dull throb and his hands went clammy.

Rows of frozen bodies.

Mul juseo.

He was almost asking her to do him a favour by taking it. But would she like it? Would it make her smile? Cry? If he threw the painting into the trees no one would ever find it. But it would still be there, with its expression and its eyes. Damn thing would probably end up back on his doorstep by morning, scare the piss out of him. Like something Raven would have done in one of his mother's stories. He almost smiled thinking about her but the stiffness of his face resisted, as if he were a child trying to contort his mouth into a gargoyle mask.

He had loved watching his mother's face when she spoke, the lines and wrinkles that started at the corners of her eyes and spilled down her cheeks into the edges of her mouth. Her skin the colour of wet cedar, her eyes so brown and deep they looked black without direct light. Eye contact with her had been like looking down a well.

"We've always had artists in the family," she'd said when he'd shown her his first painting. "And it's not just about the thing either. The painting. Art is community. It's a way for our ancestors to talk to us. It's our story."

They hadn't been as close as he'd have liked after he left the reserve to enlist. But after Korea nothing had seemed to quite work out the way it was supposed to. Like he'd shed part of his life and didn't have the energy to find it again. He'd gone through the motions, come home and married a nice girl, tried to settle down on the island near his family. And he'd made it work for a while. Long enough to get to know his son before it all went to shit and he lost himself in the military again. Made a career of it all over Canada. If he hadn't met Beth in Vancouver he probably wouldn't have retired at all. And he'd have kept painting on the side like he used to. Late at night. Posting the good ones to his son. But all of that was so long ago now. Carson was the only thing he'd held on to from his first life. That and his paintings.

His throat dried and his chest tightened. He concentrated on his feet. Marching. He stepped over a black beetle that scrambled across the tarred gravel. When he reached Irene's driveway he started to panic. What if she asked him why he'd painted it? What could he tell her?

When she answered the door he smelled fried fish and then a flowery moisturizing lotion of some kind. Irene forced half a smile, her slanting eyes wide and dark. She'd been crying. As she brushed her bangs off her forehead with her left hand, her wedding ring caught the last of the golden sunlight that had been scattered by the boughs of a cedar.

"I'm sorry to bother you." He pronounced each word care-fully, as if the reason for his visit would become obvious if he spoke slowly. "It's been a while. I'm Al, Beth's husband."

She nodded, looking down at the canvas and then back at his eyes.

Stupid of him. She knew who he was. She gave him another weak smile, as if to encourage him.

"I was at your husband's funeral."

"Yes," she said. "I know. I remember your face."

IRENE

It was like being handed a memory.

She sat on the floor with the painting leaning against the wall beside her. When Al had first shown it to her she'd gone numb, stood in the doorway staring at it, waiting for a rush of emotion to overwhelm her, but it hadn't happened. She'd felt her heart beat, heard the throb of blood in her veins as she'd retreated deep inside herself, and then it had been as if she had watched herself from above, seen her hands take the painting and close the door. Had she even thanked him? Had she told him how sorry she was about his son?

She rested her head against the cool wall. She'd imagined seeing her husband again every day since he'd died. Movie reels, black-and-white Hollywood homecomings. A man gets out of a taxi on crutches and she doesn't recognize him until he takes off his service hat. But this?

She wished she could think about her feelings in English, name them and organize them, but she had so few words to use.

She turned the canvas to face her. When she held it only a few feet away it looked almost perfect. The eyes, their exact shape, slanted less than hers because his mother wasn't Korean, and his thin straight nose, broad cheekbones and thick jaw. Al had even painted the scar on his upper lip that made him look like he was always about to smile. She traced the scar on the canvas. It made him look mischievous. Playful. The sun was setting and the image more difficult to make out now.

She pulled back her finger. The painting was still ever so slightly wet, but that wasn't what bothered her. The image wasn't smooth and something about the raised texture of the paint gave her a start, as if she were touching skin.

She rose slowly, leaving the painting on the floor, and felt dizzy as the blood ran to her feet. She leaned against the wall, not just to keep herself up but to anchor herself in the room. The sun had moved behind the trees and shadows stretched through the windows and onto the walls and floor. She shivered and flicked on a lamp, its small orange glow drawing a line in the sand, a circle that darkness couldn't cross. She stood within the light for a moment, then breathed deep and let her thoughts tumble, as if they were part of her bloodstream, circulating freely to her arms and hands and fingers, then to her legs and feet and toes.

She stepped tentatively away from the lamp and walked into the kitchen, where she began washing her dinner dishes, the smell of fish and red pepper paste pungent. One glass, one plate, one bowl.

She'd only met Al a couple of times, and they'd never really talked, but that was her fault. Beth had invited her over countless times. And she had assumed that saying no had offended Al. But the painting? Perhaps he didn't dislike her after all. Beth had stopped by a few times a week since it had happened, even the day after Al's son had gone missing. She was good to her. A good friend. Or was she just a good neighbour? Was there a difference in Canada?

She left the dishes to air-dry on the wooden rack beside the sink and wiped her hands on a dishtowel. She picked up a bottle of moisturizing cream and spread it over her hands. Her mother had mailed it to her. The air became heavy with the scent, a hint of bitter green tea leaves touching her tongue as she breathed. She lifted her shirt and ran her moist hands over her belly and abdomen, rubbing the excess cream into the small red and dark purple stretch marks, each like a border drawn on a map.

She walked back into the living room and tried not to look at the painting. She closed her eyes and tested herself. She could picture his face easily, see the lines across his forehead, three of them, and his short black hair that he always let grow when he was off-duty. But would her memories of his face and voice and touch slowly erode, fade, disappear? The thought terrified her. Maybe it would be harder for her to forget what he looked like now that she had the painting. She didn't have many photos, only a wedding album and a few from before they were married. She'd always felt conscious of people seeing her as another Asian tourist with a camera. Usually she just kept pictures of people she didn't see often. She should have known better with a husband in the military. It had only been a matter of time before he was called off somewhere.

She'd been taught in school to revere the men who'd come to fight for the South. They'd come from all over the world. Turkey, England, Canada. But all anyone ever talked about was the Americans. Probably because they'd never left. The Canadians had though. She wished she had asked Al questions about Korea and about the portrait, that she hadn't been so shy, so caught off guard.

So surprised.

She translated into English and her thoughts stumbled.

If Joseph were here, he would have helped her find the right words.

She looked down at the painting. In the dim light from the lamp in the corner of the room the portrait took on an ethereal glow, the oil shining.

Her lower back ached and she leaned to each side and then backwards, flexing her hips. Usually the baby kicked after dinner. Her neck muscles tensed. She put her hands on her stomach and rubbed it slowly, trying to think of reasons why the baby might not be moving. Did babies kick at the same time every day? She had read so many books that she could hardly keep any of it straight. And some of the Korean books conflicted with the English ones, and then there were so many new words to learn. She could call her mother, but then, if something was wrong, she would still be alone. And she could call Beth, but Al might answer and she knew she wouldn't be able to find the right words.

Perhaps it was better to wait. Wasn't that what pregnant women did?

Maybe she was just so used to the kicks and bumps she hadn't noticed them. And didn't the baby usually kick more in the morning?

Just having the painting calmed her, helped her to refocus her thoughts. She turned off the lamp and stood in the dark until her eyes adjusted. Through the sliding glass doors the sunset faded slowly, orange and pink and blue through wisps of cloud, and a sliver moon rose over the trees. Soon stars would cast thin pricks of light towards her, and outside her house a different stirring would begin, calm, like the practised movements of the blind. Bat wings. The rustle of raccoons in the huckleberry bush. The rote swivel of an owl's head.

Did ants sleep? The world seemed to change at night and perhaps she did too. She felt more alone. Was it the darkness or was it just because she was so tired?

She tried to imagine each of the houses along Deloume Road. Reading lamps on, the glow of television sets and the rise and fall of muffled conversations over coffee or tea. She stood up on her tiptoes to stretch the muscles in her feet and ankles and felt her full weight. Her world had changed so quickly, moved so fast, and she was too heavy to keep up with it.

She cracked the sliding door open an inch, breathed the fresh air, cool against her warm face. She heard the undulating hoot of an owl and she opened the door wider. Stars appeared for her and she stared straight into their light, not through the glass, but face to face.

AL HENRY

He loaded the gun and slipped out of the house, walking through the falling dark in the direction of the stop sign.

MATTHEW

The low sun cast rich light through the canopy of leaves over the old car wreck. He tried six of the seven keys in the lock of the glove compartment. None of them worked.

He didn't know why he was surprised.

Darkness crept out from the trees around him. His father's voice echoed through the forest from the back door of the house, calling him home for the night. The forest's greens faded to grey and blue, then blue to black, and crickets started up. A shadow passed silently overhead.

There could be anything in there.

Dry ferns moved at his feet and he stepped onto the old floorboards of the car, his eyes straining to see what crawled towards him. His mind raced as his father's voice boomed through the growing shadows again.

He and his brother had camped in these same woods last summer. The tent had sagged and collapsed on them, and his brother had almost wet himself laughing. And he'd shown him how to make shadow puppets, Andy trying so hard at first, then getting frustrated, staring at his own hands in the dim light, willing them to take shape, become graceful, winged, alive.

He remembered waking up in the drooping tent. The light had been different, pale at first, then brighter through the dew and condensation that ran down the roof and sides of the tent, the beads catching and scattering the early morning rays. Later their mom had hung the sleeping bags and tent to air-dry on wooden deck chairs, the summer heat dulling the fabrics, and he'd watched white moths, clumsy through the air, passing over the blue nylon and canvas.

A gunshot cracked and echoed in the distance, then another, and, just as the sound faded, a third.

Was someone hunting at night?

One key left.

In the dark the car wreck became a monstrosity, jagged metal teeth above and below him, the dark interior a throat. Another rustle beneath the car. Snake? He extended his hand slowly, the key shaking, then paused in front of the lock, fingers outstretched, heart pounding, and his father's voice growing sharper, calling him home.

JOSH

He stood behind Matthew in the half hush between day and night, impressed with himself for being able to get so close undetected. His friend's hand hung in the air in front of the glove compartment of the old car. Matthew's dad was yelling for him to come home to bed and he knew that his mother was probably doing the same farther up the road. He wished he lived with Matthew and Andy sometimes. With parents who didn't fight so much.

He hesitated, waiting to see if the key would work this time. Shadows grew upside-down from branches and his neck prickled as the forest adjusted to the darkness just like he would in his bedroom, breathing out heavily to hear himself, wiggling deeper beneath his blankets.

He stepped forward and a twig crunched beneath his foot. Matthew stood up quickly and swivelled around, smacking his head on the door frame.

"It's me," said Josh.

"Whadda ya doing sneaking up like that?"

"Sorry. Did I scare you?"

"No," said Matthew, rubbing his head.

"I tried to open it once," said Josh. "But I didn't have a key and then I kinda forgot about it."

Matthew's father yelled again, louder. The crickets went silent, then started over from the beginning.

"Are you gonna try it?" asked Josh, thinking about what his mom would say if he stayed much longer.

Matthew slid the key into the lock and tried to turn it. It wouldn't budge.

"It doesn't fit," said Matthew. "Forget it, I gotta go."

"Wait. What if I just hit the lock with something?"

He picked up a fallen branch. Matthew stepped aside and Josh hammered the glove compartment, the end of the branch breaking off with the impact. The tiny door flopped open. He dropped the stick.

"I can't believe that worked," he said.

Neither of them had a flashlight.

"You check inside," said Matthew.

He hesitated. "Why me?"

"We'll share whatever we find."

He thought about the aluminum-handled hockey stick they shared in Matthew's basement, and the Green Lantern comics they shared in Matthew's bedroom.

"Come on," said Matthew. "Just reach in and grab it. There's probably nothing there anyway."

Josh leaned inside the car. It smelled like an overturned log. Musty. Becoming dirt. He glanced at his friend and reached in.

ANDY

He tucked the green fleece blanket under the mattress of the top bunk and let the blanket fall, enclosing the bed beneath. The beds were in the corner of the room and he draped another blanket off the end.

Safe. Hiding.

His father's voice boomed outside the bedroom window.

He held a yellow plastic flashlight, and he flicked it on and off. He slipped through the blanket and crawled onto the bottom bunk. Darkness. Pillow and sheets swirled into a pile. Back against the wall. Feet under the sheet.

Be quiet.

He turned on the flashlight. Blue and red cars on his bed-sheets. He wriggled his toes. Moving cars.

He shone the flashlight on the green fleece blanket. Images like a movie. Camping with Matthew. The tent falling over. Laughing. Dark night in a droopy tent by the well. Noises without faces. He sucked in a deep breath.

His dad's voice from outside again.

Keys. Stop following.

Flashlight beam on the tent's wall. His brother's fingers. Rabbit and fox. Butterfly.

He closed his eyes and let the flashlight rest on his knee.

The smell of nylon sleeping bags. The sound of the broom's bristles sweeping twigs and leaves and dead bugs from the tent floor.

Bugs.

He listened for his brother's footsteps on the stairs.

He opened his eyes and fumbled with the flashlight in one hand, trying to form animals with his other in front of the small bulb, but he couldn't make it work.

Two. Two hands.

He tried to prop the flashlight up on a blanket and form animals with both hands, but his fingers wouldn't listen.

The bedroom door handle turned and he clicked off the flashlight. Held his breath.

"Andy, honey?" came his mother's voice. "Have you seen your brother?"

He exhaled. "Keys," he said.

His mom sighed and shut the door. Flashlight on again. Bulb getting darker. He looked straight at its glowing filaments, closed his eyes and saw spots and colours, hazily electric. Bright.

Waking and looking up at patterns of moving light on the tent's roof. Leaves. Birds. Good noises.

A door closed downstairs and his father's deep voice rose and fell in muffled tones. Then silence. The house creaked and breathed through open doors and windows.

Flashlight off. Eyes adjusting. Grey forms. Blankets hiding him.

Downstairs his father's voice rose sharply and stopped. The house sighed and Andy shifted his feet beneath the sheets. Footsteps up the stairs. The bedroom door opened and closed. Feet up the rungs to the top bunk. The bed groaned.

"Hey Andy," his brother whispered. "You still awake?"

April, 1899

He sat on the mattress, the iron cot squeaking as the springs sank. He'd given the rain five days before packing up his tent and heading for the mill town, a full day's walk from the lightning-singed Douglas fir—the promised land behind him for the time being. He'd planted apple seeds around the scorched tree on a whim, and he wondered if the rains would wash them out. Already the streets here were rivers of mud, boards set like tightrope wires for sidewalks.

A knock at his door. He stood and opened it and in came the matron of the boarding house, broad, like two women stuck together at the shoulders, with grey hair coming loose in wild strands from a bun behind her head.

"Some sheets and towels Mr. Deloume." She left them folded on a wooden chair and made her exit as swiftly as she'd come.

Rain tapped at the window like a conductor's baton on a music stand. He stared through the glass out over the brown street. No cobblestones like Victoria had, thank God. Enough noise there from the streetcars to deafen you. Crowding like London. Layer on layer of filth. It was why he'd left. And Lord, he was a long way from home and his sister now. Although the mud reminded him of growing up on the farm.

His mother's swollen belly and him just a boy. *A pumpkin growing inside me, love.* And he'd asked her why she didn't make it stop. *Too late, son.* Then his sister had been born and the pumpkin's toothless cries had terrified him until she'd grown to look human. Together on the farm, laughing, tin can to can on a string through the garden. He imagined a giant string, long enough to cross North America and the Atlantic.

Don't go Gerard. Canada's not safe. You can stay with us here.

Elizabeth was married now. Their family farm long gone and she in London. He took out the compass she'd given him as a parting gift, the silver case engraved with his initials. He hadn't written her in months. But she had her concerns at home. Two children of her own now. When he did write he omitted anything that might scare her or make her worry. He'd told her of the giant trees but not of the stumps torn to shreds by mountain lions sharpening their claws, the smallpox that killed off damn near all the Natives, the scattered bones of missing loggers and surveyors he came across from time to time. Just one slip off a windfall, one broken ankle or falling tree limb. This land wasn't for everyone. But it was for him. Just the space and freedom. The time to think, to see a world that hadn't been smothered by soot and thousands upon thousands of hungry mouths. A place where the Lord's voice still echoed from His creation.

Lightning and the tree bursting into flames, sparks falling like rain.

There was a bible on his bed, and he found Exodus. The story of Moses. The burning bush. The Promised Land.

He clutched the compass tight and the heat from his hand made the metal feel soft, as though it might melt and slide off his palm onto the bed.

Wind drove the rain sideways into the windowpane in staccato as he took out his sketchbook, unbinding the loose sheets and scanning them. He had time to kill now. Had to dry out properly or he'd stay wet and catch his death. He could hear loggers and mill workers downstairs in the common area playing cards and laughing. Loud as all hell. He'd stick to his room. Paid extra for privacy. Bad enough to be inside and away from the woods in spring, wet as it was now. Damned if he wasn't restless already. He got up and opened the window for some fresh air, the wind howling through the room with unexpected force, sending the loose papers from his sketchbook swirling overhead. He stood still, mouth open, watching the soaring paper, each piece turning and hanging in the air as if attached to the ceiling by invisible strings.

The Leaf

A single thread of spider's web hangs from a maple branch with a small alder leaf attached, light green and dry brown, its edges curled so it looks like a cocoon. It hangs a few feet above the road, and when moving clouds cover the sun, the thread becomes invisible and the leaf hangs in mid-air.

We crouch beside it and watch as it sways and twists in the gentle breeze.

'"When a car comes it'll wreck it," I say, glancing over my shoulder, waiting for the sound of an engine.

A breeze picks up speed and the leaf sways like a pendulum. The clouds shift and sunlight filters through the canopy of late summer leaves, turning the silky gloss of the spider's web silver.

"No one wanted it to happen," I say. "We didn't mean it."

Your skin bloodless, cold.

You continue to stare at the leaf without speaking, as though watching it keep time in the wind, your features blurring in the play of sun and shade, your outline small and fragile beside me, ready to disappear the moment I blink.

JONAH DAVIES

His truck's tires bumped from the ferry's metal plank onto the dock and he accelerated, leaving the terminal in Nanaimo behind and heading south down Vancouver Island towards Mill Bay. What was it about arriving on the island, about passing over water from Vancouver, leaving the continent behind? Felt like he was heading towards the edge of the world. He laughed at himself. To hell with it. Just another place. His grandsons'd be happy to see him. Even if Avril wouldn't.

MILES FORD

He woke early and opened the door, the shed filling with the sun's dull morning rays. He looked back at the wool blanket but didn't fold it. His jaw stretched and tightened into a yawn. He let the door bang shut behind him, then unzipped his pants and pissed until steam rose from the ground.

He wasn't sure what the butcher would think about him sleeping in the shed, but the door had been unlocked and there'd been a blanket on the floor. He'd noticed the shed the night before and anywhere was better than going home. His hand was just starting to heal and he touched the beginnings of a scab across his palm. He walked onto Deloume Road and stopped to look back at the pig farm. The butcher would be awake soon but he didn't want to talk to him. It was too awkward and the man's thick accent and watering eyes bothered him. Miles tried to think what was wrong with them. Sometimes they were blood-shot, but it wasn't that, it was more how the butcher looked at him, as if he expected him to say something important.

He walked across the road and waded through the grass to the fence of the cow pasture. It was easy as nothing to be a cow. He watched a black-and-white meander drunkenly out of a barn towards a patch of grass. The sky was brightening by the minute and Miles fingered the barbed wire of the fence, picking at the rust with his fingernail. The air smelled empty and clean, as though it were ready to be filled. His breathing was shallow and his chest tight. It was the same when he tried to run. Like his lungs got smaller with each breath, like they would shrink into nothing and leave him suffocating even with air all around him. It seemed to be getting a bit worse every day and now his nose wouldn't clear at night, forcing him to breathe through his mouth.

Over the river and past the stop sign. The metal sign looked brighter, new, and even the bullet holes through the O were cleaner and smaller than he remembered. He kept walking until he reached his parents' driveway, his feet balancing on the invisible line between driveway and road. Piles of stripped tires and sheets of weathered aluminum siding led to the old trailer. How did they live there? It wasn't a place for people.

The sun was up now and pieces of metal shone along the edges of the driveway. The Doberman watched him from behind a faded blue car door that seemed to stand without leaning, as though it had taken root. The dog's pointed black ears stood still and it fixed its eyes on him. He ignored the dog and looked down at the pothole at his feet, its dry, rough edges crumbling a few inches in front of his shoes. He imagined the hole full of water and his reflection in it, his own muddy eyes staring back up at him, his brown matted hair. The image disappeared as a car engine hacked to life up the road. The dog stiffened, its ears following the sound.

He stepped over the pothole and walked halfway up the driveway. Could they see him from inside the trailer? Had they even noticed he was gone? He tried to imagine how different it would be without him there but stopped short as the dog stood up and dragged its chain to the middle of the driveway. He wondered if the dog would run away if it weren't chained.

There was a murmur of voices from the trailer. He pictured what it looked like inside. Empty walls. Fake wood cupboards. Tidy and bare, completely the opposite of the mess outside. He walked closer to the metal house, listening to his parents' voices inside, their words tinny as they argued. Were they talking about him? His dad's voice bellowed and something crashed and broke on the trailer floor. A mug or a plate.

The Doberman paced in front of the trailer, its chain sliding through the gravel and mud. The dog sniffed the purple oily water and lifted its head, looking first at the trailer then down the driveway towards Deloume.

Miles turned and followed the dog's gaze with his feet.

SAM TOEWS

The bone-light of dawn filled the sky. He watched through a gap in the blackberry bushes as Miles emerged from a shed on the pig farm across the road and pissed on a fence post.

So, the butcher had company.

Sam knelt beside his vegetable garden. He'd been checking the chicken-wire fence for holes. Sometimes he wondered if rabbits and deer actually chewed through the metal to get to the carrots and lettuce. Sweet peas climbed up one side of the fence and the leaves that poked through the wire had been eaten too.

He watched the boy walk down Deloume and out of sight. The butcher lived alone. And the boy was, what, ten? Could be bad news. People wouldn't like it. He didn't want to think it of the butcher though. Something about his thick accent made him an underdog, and Lord knew he always bet on the dark horse.

A hint of blue was beginning to show as the sun's pale yellow deepened. Patching up the fence probably wasn't worth his time. Best just to find a new roll of chicken wire. Bob Ford would have some. Should he tell Bob that he'd seen Miles? Hard one. Could get the butcher into a crapload of trouble he didn't deserve. But Bob was the boy's father and that counted for something. If it were Sam's boy he'd want to know. Bob was a hard man though, and it didn't take much imagination to guess why Miles wasn't living at home. Damn it all. How was it a man like Bob ended up married and raising a family?

It'd be easier to deal with things like this if he had a wife to talk to. Someone with a knack for people problems. Give him a cow and he'd know how to deal with just about anything. But families? Maybe he was better off without kids.

It wouldn't feel right to go to Bob about it. But he'd have to talk to the butcher. At least let him know what he was getting himself into. Foreign man living alone, boy staying on the property. Sounded bad. Looked bad.

Yep, Bob was a hard man. Sam wouldn't want to go nose to nose with him. Not again. But that had been years ago. Back when they'd been teenagers. Water under the bridge. Not that he'd ever shy from a scrap if it came his way, but there was no need to bring hell down on you. No need at all.

MATTHEW

He woke in his clothes. In his right hand beneath the pillow he clutched the compass, its metal flip-top case warm from his hand. He placed it on his pillow. There was a small clasp where a chain or a string could be attached, and engraved on the outside of the round metal were the letters G and D.

As he opened it the hinges shuddered, rasping like a baby crow. He'd stolen a glance at it the night before in the porch light outside his house, but his father had been so angry with him for being late that he hadn't dared keep his bedroom light on. And Andy had killed the flashlight batteries again.

The compass wobbled inside the glass and then corrected a few degrees so the needle pointed straight at his chest. The four directions were painted in red calligraphy on the yellowing surface, the degrees in black. Just looking at it gave him shivers. His very own hidden treasure. He sat up, twisted around and held the compass in front of him so that he could look north. His gaze followed the needle right into the blue eyes of his brother, who stood on the bunk-bed ladder peering at him.

"Jeez Andy, how long have you been watching? You scared the—"

"See you," said Andy, biting his lip and grinning that goofy little smile. His eyes had fallen on the compass and Matthew could see his mouth forming the word *watch*.

"Come up here for a minute," he said, patting the mattress beside him. Andy hesitated, then climbed the rest of the ladder and sat down on the top bunk. He was wearing a pair of his old hand-me-down racing car pyjamas.

"Watch," said Andy.

Matthew shook his head. "Compass," he said, rotating the disc in his hand so Andy could see that the needle never stopped facing the same direction. "North," said Matthew, pointing at the wall.

Andy nodded, his blue eyes wide and his mouth shut tight.

Matthew twisted around and held out the compass so it faced the wall beside their bed.

"North," said Andy, pointing the direction they were facing.

Matthew shook his head again and let Andy lean over to see the needle pointing back in the original direction. "North's always that way from here," he said.

Andy looked at the needle then over his shoulder north, swallowing loud enough to hear. It was a signal that he was being patient, that he didn't understand and that he was waiting to touch the compass. Matthew laughed and took his brother's hand, placing the compass in his palm. Andy held it like a bowl of water, turning slowly so his whole body faced north.

If their father saw the compass he might take it away. The first thing his dad would ask was where he'd found it, and Matthew wasn't great at lying. Besides, his dad had a way of knowing, and the last thing he wanted was to have to take it back to the Fords' place and explain what he and Josh had done.

"North," said his brother.

And now that Andy knew, it was only a matter of time before he wandered off to show it to their parents. His brother wouldn't mean to spill the secret but it would happen, as usual.

He watched Andy close the lid and reopen it slowly, peering through the smallest crack as if to surprise the compass sleeping and catch it facing the wrong direction.

Footsteps sounded in the hallway and dishes clattered on the kitchen counter downstairs.

He could hide it, but that would only work for a little while. It was frustrating. His parents would never take something from Andy if he was attached to it. Sometimes he felt like he got punished for being normal. Maybe his parents wouldn't care, but a compass seemed grown-up, something his dad would keep in the off-limits top drawer of his dresser, along with his Swiss Army knife, tobacco pipe and the razor-sharp letter opener that missionary friends had sent from Papua New Guinea.

"North," said Andy again.

It wasn't fair . . . He slid past his brother and down the ladder. In the back of their closet under a pile of old Halloween costumes he found a pair of running shoes that were too small for either of them. He pulled the green lace out of one and held it up. It was long enough. Next he took the compass from Andy, who had climbed down after him. He pushed one end of the shoelace through the compass's metal clasp then tied the ends of the shoelace together so the compass hung like a pendant on a necklace. Josh wasn't going to be happy about it, especially after letting him take it home first, but if he didn't do something they'd never get to use it at all.

"Present," he said to Andy, hanging the compass around his brother's neck.

Andy stood for a moment with his hands at his sides. He blinked and stared at Matthew's chest as if he didn't understand, or as if by moving he might ruin the moment and the compass around his neck might disappear. Then he raised his hands slowly and held the compass to his chest.

"I?" he said.

Matthew nodded and laughed as his brother started to bounce and giggle, holding the crotch of his pyjamas with one hand.

"Go to the bathroom," he said, pushing Andy gently towards the door and steering him down the hall to the bathroom.

Matthew watched him go and wondered if it would work. His brother might lose the compass, but there was no way their parents would force a tantrum by taking it away from him, and Andy couldn't be expected to explain where it had come from. He heard his brother pissing in the toilet and then on the seat, and he imagined him dropping the compass in the yellow water. He heard a flush and the tap running, then his brother's high, excited voice.

"North."

ANDY

He leaned forward over his Cheerios, his chest pressed against the edge of the table, pinning the shoelace. The string tugged against the back of his neck. The compass dangled beneath the table. He gripped his spoon and looked at his parents sitting across from him. Eyes watching. He scooped up Cheerios and milk and bit down, milk running out of the corners of his mouth as he chewed.

He heard his mother's voice. Broken tones. Then a damp cloth scrubbed his cheeks and the corners of his mouth. He turned his head from side to side to avoid the cloth.

"No," he said. "No."

"Just let him eat," came his father's voice.

And then it faded to a tone too, a rumbling bass sinking under the table and chairs.

He finished eating and stood up, wiping his mouth on his pyjama sleeve. His bare feet stuck to the eggshell linoleum and he looked down at sunlight in the shape of a window warming a patch of floor. He stepped into it. Warm toes.

His parents were talking again and he looked at his mom.

"I just don't have the energy today," she said.

He turned his head and watched his dad's mouth.

"Oh just let him keep it then. Remember what happened when I took away that balloon at the fair . . ."

He wrapped his fingers around the compass. His parents' voices hummed as he opened it and held it out, his fingers trembling so much that he had to cup it in both hands. The needle pointed at his parents and he shuffled his feet so his shoulders were square with them. He closed the lid and tried again. And again.

His parents stood watching him, the needle pointing straight at them.

His dad leaned down and kissed his cheek. Aftershave.

". . . work now," said his dad.

He watched the compass to see which of his parents the needle would follow when his dad left.

June, 1899

Spring to early summer and he stood again at the tall Douglas fir, his compass swinging from his neck. Days of mosquitoes and deer paths just to find the logging trail that ran through the valley again after surveying for coal and minerals farther inland and north. The trail was being reclaimed by bracken fern, salal and cedar saplings. And the area was wetter than years past. More insects. Less sun. Still, he'd been drawn back. Called even in his sleep. Lightning when he closed his eyes. Bark to ash. Insects ablaze.

He walked away from the tree farther into the small valley, the path and forest around him dark shades of green beneath the branches of hemlock and cedar.

Whistle-lisp of thrush, crow-throat caw, rustle of rabbit unseen beneath fern and nettle. He stopped and stood as still as he could. Everything moved, breathed and shifted, each moss-covered log and wet bough, each tree with a secret name long forgotten—Adam's whispers in Eden before the Fall. Wildflower, red cedar, lichen art on bark. Lighting through darkness into thought.

The trees had names that were forever, roots deep in the soil. And the soil had a name, and the water, and the spinning earth too, with a memory that would remain untouched until the end of time. How long would he have to stand here to take root, until his veins ran with earth water, until he grew in the sunlight, until his skin turned to bark tough enough to weather the seasons and block out the droning mosquitoes in his ears? New fern had a name too, and dandelion and baby raven. Their names had meanings that couldn't be separated from the earth. He hated the thought of leaving this place again. Of more work up north. He needed to find a way to stay. To lay down roots in the promised land. To leave the rest behind forever.

A pumpkin growing inside me, love.

I'm worried about you Gerard. Alone in the woods. When are you coming home?

Tin cans on a string.

A grey jay landed beside him and hopped to his feet, then flapped to a branch above. He took bread from his canvas sack and broke it, holding out a tiny piece. The jay swooped from the branch and took the crumb quickly, its wings barely brushing his fingers. He held out another piece and a second jay landed on his hand, its small talons hooking into his palm without breaking the skin. It took the bread and cocked its head to look at him.

"I know your secret name, friend. It's Beg."

He slogged his way along the disappearing trail through wet, waist-high ferns and fallen branches until he reached a small clearing of stumps, each wide as a cart and still ten feet high, with springboard slots cut into them. The first loggers through had taken some of the largest trees for masts, but the valley was too far from the coast for them to have bothered with the rest yet. There was still more than enough lumber nearer the water and sawmill. Miles of it. Enough to last forever perhaps. Sunlight poured into the clearing and he looked up, caught sight of an eagle circling. It straightened its path and glided ahead of him and out of sight. And he knew its name too. Mapmaker, compass of the sky.

Ferns and underbrush gave off moisture as they shone in the sharp, wet light. Leaves glistened and cedar boughs rustled, dropping water in the breeze.

MATTHEW

He let Josh go first as they crossed the small ditch and made their way through the underbrush. The broom was thick, and dry black pods fell from the upright stems as they pushed through them. Above, a bald eagle circled and landed on the scorched crown of the giant Douglas fir. They stumbled through the bush to the fence along the dairy farm where apple trees grew. The ground was clearer there, and covered with anemic grass, a few strawberry vines and five or six rotting apples that had fallen and not yet been carried away by birds.

Josh picked an apple from a tree and rubbed it on his shirt before biting into it, his face turning inside out.

Matthew laughed.

"It tastes good," said Josh. "Try one."

Matthew shook his head, kneeling down to pick a wild strawberry. "These look sweet," he said, as Josh threw his half-eaten apple into the woods. Matthew tried the strawberry. It was still sour but he didn't make a face.

"Why didn't you just hide it?" asked Josh.

"I told you. 'Cause my dad might've found it and taken it away. They never take anything off of Andy."

"I knew I should've taken it. My parents wouldn't have even noticed."

Josh was right. He should've let him take the compass. Even if he did break things sometimes. Matthew leaned against the tree, looking up its trunk. He wondered if the eagle was watching them with its eyes that could see fish beneath the surface of water.

"I wish I had four eyelids," he said.

"Huh?" Josh tried one of the strawberries, grimaced and spat it out.

"Eagles can see when they blink. One set of eyelids is clear."

Josh shrugged. "My dad says a tail feather's worth a lot. Maybe we can find one to sell."

Matthew shook his head. "You don't sell them."

"How come?" asked Josh.

"Because they're special." Wind rudder, he thought. The secret of flight.

Josh swore as he stubbed his toe, turning up grass and moss. Matthew reached down and picked up a rusted iron tent peg.

"How long's that been there do you think?" asked Josh.

"Looks old," said Matthew, dropping the tent peg as they continued to circle the massive tree looking for eagle feathers.

"I wish I had eagle eyes," said Josh. "If you could have any superpower what would you pick?"

Matthew stopped and looked up at the tree again. "Time travel," he said.

"Aw, that always gets messed up," said Josh. "You'd probably get stuck someplace you didn't wanna be. Like in a dinosaur's cave or something."

"Yeah, maybe," said Matthew. "Josh, when you remember stuff, can you smell it?"

"Whadda ya mean?"

"I don't know. Like, if you think about a place, is it like going there?"

"Hey! Look at this! I found one," said Josh, holding up a tattered crow's feather.

Matthew smiled as the hum of insects filled the air around them.

AVRIL

She watched Bob Ford load his truck, a large black Chevy that had been spray-painted so its matte surface seemed to absorb light. He'd started a couple of hours later than she'd hoped, but at least he'd come. She felt a twinge of guilt for getting rid of so much, but it wasn't like she was selling family heirlooms. The old lawn mower had sat in the garage untouched for almost two years. And Matthew had been making noises about wanting to play road hockey on the cement floor for months now.

Bob's stocky frame moved with a grace and precision that surprised her. He hardly seemed to have broken a sweat and he lifted the rolls of wire fence as though they were pillows. He was clearly used to working alone.

"Bob," she said, "I don't mean to interrupt, but did you get a chance to talk to Miles about coming over sometime?"

He grunted, leaned on his truck and stared at her, then brushed past her back into the garage and wheeled the lawn mower to his truck.

"I was just thinking that he might be bored. You know how kids get this time of year. "

Bob laughed roughly, the sound tearing on his yellow teeth as it left his mouth.

She took a step back and crossed her arms.

"You obviously haven't spent any time with mine," said Bob. "They take after their mother." He hauled the lawn mower up into the back of his truck. "Heads in the clouds. Happy to sit on their asses any time of year."

Avril stared at him, trying not to frown. "Well, anyway. I just thought Miles might be looking for something to do."

Bob spat. He climbed down from the truck and pointed at the garage. She turned to look at all the empty space.

"That's it then," he said, sniffing and putting his thick hands on his hips.

"Right. Thanks." She was sick of trying now, annoyed at his avoidance, but she didn't want to give up. "So, was Miles just not interested?"

"Haven't seen him." He stared back at her, oddly expressionless.

"You mean since we last spoke?" she asked, regretting the words instantly.

He turned his back on her and walked to his truck, opening the cab door and fishing out a worn brown leather wallet. He thumbed through some bills.

"Fifty-five, then?" he said, holding out a fistful of fives and tens.

JONAH DAVIES

He turned off the ignition and listened to the engine simmer under the hood. The house looked more lived-in than when he'd last seen it—flower boxes in the upstairs windows, white trim in bright contrast to the stained, bevelled cedar siding, bikes lying next to a small wooden shed. The front lawn was less patchy, still brown in places though. The kids were in the small carport with the garage door open, playing hockey on the only patch of cement for miles. Andy was in goal, a four-litre ice cream pail for a helmet and a baseball mitt for a catcher. Matthew held an old, taped-up wooden stick a foot taller than he was. Both boys stared at him through the truck's window.

He opened the door and stepped out, the heels of his boots digging into the loose gravel. He left the door open to air out the cab. The boys didn't move. The pail fell over Andy's eyes and the boy left it there. Finally Matthew leaned the stick against the wall and stepped out of the shaded garage.

"Grandpa?" said the boy.

"Well who the hell else is it gonna be?" he said, taking out his pipe and filling it.

Matthew stared at him for another moment, squinting, then turned and ran inside, yelling for his mother. The boy'd grown like a weed over the past year or so. Barely recognized him. His hair was turning reddish like his mom's and he looked strong and healthy, not a hint of frailty about him. More than he could say for Andy.

Andy put his hands in front of him and took a few steps forward, then turned in a circle, the plastic pail still over his eyes. A metal locket swung from his neck on a shoelace.

Jonah lit a match and held it to the tobacco in his pipe, looking down his nose at the loose strands as they twisted and burned. He reached inside the cab and grabbed his Stetson. Hot as hell out. He smoked and waited, leaning against the dusty blue pickup.

Matthew pulled her outside by the hand. She hadn't changed much. She stood with the two boys behind her, staring at him.

"Aren't you gonna say nothing?" he asked.

"You can't smoke in the house, Dad," she said.

"Ain't in the house, Avril."

Andy walked past his brother and mom, his hands still out in front of him, the pail wobbling with each step, until he bumped into the truck.

"You remember your grandpa, Andy?" he asked.

Andy tilted his head back so he could see out from under the bucket. "Hot," he said, pointing at the pipe.

Jonah laughed, the phlegm in his throat catching, turning it into a cough.

"You didn't call," said Avril.

"Figured you'd be around."

"Jesus, Dad, it's a two-day drive. What if we'd been away?"

He shrugged, breathing in the rich smoke and exhaling the tension of the road.

"Did you bring us anything Grandpa?" asked Matthew.

His mother sighed and frowned.

Jonah smiled. "In the back. Why don't you and your brother help this old man with his luggage. That is, if your mother's gonna let me inside."

"Oh Dad. Just leave the pipe outside." She turned and walked briskly into the house.

"I like the smell of it Grandpa," said Matthew.

"Yeah, me too," he said, patting the boy on the head. He walked around to the back of the truck and pulled out a small green suitcase and a brown paper bag. The suitcase was worn and stained and covered with stickers. One from each province and state he'd taken it to.

He put the suitcase on the ground beside Matthew. "Reckon you can handle it?"

Matthew nodded and picked it up with both hands, walking awkwardly towards the house.

Jonah handed the paper bag to Andy. "Follow your brother with this," he said, pointing at Matthew.

Andy took the bag and ran inside. Jonah exhaled slowly, letting the smoke curl in front of his eyes and around the bottom of his hat's brim. He shut the door of the truck and followed the kids, stopping for one last draw on his pipe before leaving it to burn down slowly on a window ledge beside the open garage.

He took off his hat and contemplated heading inside.

Well, at least he wouldn't have to sleep in his truck.

AVRIL

She sat at the table watching the boys eat halved apples with raisins stuffed into their cored centres.

"Did you see his licence plates Mom?" asked Matthew. "Alberta. Wild Rose Country."

She nodded.

"Are there really wild roses in Alberta?"

She nodded again.

"Everywhere? Just wild?"

She sighed and tried to smile. "Just in some places," she said.

"Wow. I wanna go to Alberta. Can I?"

She raised her eyebrow. What was she supposed to say? If she said yes he'd take it as a promise, and unlike Andy, or even Josh, he wasn't the type of kid to forget.

"We'll see," she said. "Finish your snack."

Her dad was upstairs showering. He could have at least called first. But she knew what she would have told him—that they were too busy with the boys—and, well, now here he was. She'd barely spoken to him since her mom died last year. She didn't mean to blame him. But here he was, still smoking and still so . . . *alive*.

David would be pleased though. He'd always liked her dad. Even if he was a redneck. His word, not hers.

"Did you see his hat and cowboy boots? Is Grandpa a cowboy?"

"Not quite," she said.

She watched Andy's focus as he ate, the way he examined each raisin before putting it into his mouth. Couldn't have had less similar kids. But things were getting easier as they got older. And at least they were getting along this summer. Andy was growing up in his way. Fewer tantrums. A bit more social.

She glanced at Matthew. His eyes were wide, flitting around the room. It was almost a relief to see him so excited. Not quite so grown-up. He was different than other ten-year-olds. Thoughtful, always planning ahead. Part of it was because of Andy. He was becoming more and more protective of him. Learning how to talk to him, how to communicate without getting completely frustrated all the time, like he had when they'd been younger. It was a good thing, and she was relieved not to have to watch Andy so closely any more, but sometimes she wished Matthew didn't have to carry that unexpected responsibility, that he could just let himself go a little, get more into the moment—be a kid. Like Josh. Of course, Josh also broke just about everything he touched.

Matthew saw her watching. "How come you don't like Grandpa's pipe?"

"Hot," said Andy, chewing a raisin and then spitting it out on the table.

"Andy, honey, no," she said. "Swallow please."

Andy laughed and gulped dramatically.

"Is it the smell?" asked Matthew.

"Yes, it's the smell," she answered. "And it's bad for you."

"How bad?"

"I . . . it's very bad . . . it's . . ." She pictured her mother, frail and still, and again the thought that it shouldn't have been her took hold. That it should have been him. All the drinking and smoking.

"Like whisky?" Matthew interrupted her thoughts. "Josh's uncle drinks whisky and his mom says he's goodfornothing."

"Yes, a bit like whisky. But it makes breathing harder."

Matthew stared down at the table, as if reading the grain of the pine surface. "Is it gonna kill him?"

She stood up. "It might," she said. "One day."

IRENE

She took off her clothes and ran a bath, sitting heavily on the toilet beside the tub. She'd already lost count of how many times she'd peed that day, and she imagined the baby squeezing her bladder with its tiny hands.

Her belly covered half of her thighs as she sat and waited for the bath to fill. She fingered her popped-out belly button and traced the stretch marks running down from it over her abdomen. In the small of her back a slow ache spread up and down and she twisted slightly on the seat, trying to relieve it.

The bath was half full and the water looked thick and glossy inside the shiny white porcelain. She transferred her rear to the edge of the tub and dipped her fingers into the hot water. When she turned off the tap the silence of the room surprised her. Drops of water fell from the nozzle into the clear water. She lifted one leg slowly and stepped into the bath, then the other, sliding down, her knee joints cracking and her arms straining on the edges for balance.

Her stomach was a cartoon island, round and smooth. Her breasts had swollen too, and she allowed herself a smile, her chapped lips pulling taut. She'd always wanted breasts like this. Only not so tender. She turned her head slowly from side to side, working at the stiffness in her neck. Why was her neck stiff? Wasn't it enough that she was exhausted and that the rest of her ached?

Her fingers were swelling in the heat and she slipped off her silver wedding band and put it on the edge of the tub. She'd put it on for the first time less than nine months ago. She stared at the wet silver, stark against white. Beth had asked her once what her maiden name was, and when she'd responded "Choi," Beth hadn't understood, and had told her how she hadn't wanted to take Al's name, how "Henry" just sounded too strange and how she was too attached to her maiden name, although everyone called her Mrs. Henry anyway. Irene had managed to explain that her maiden name was Choi too, and that she hadn't changed it either.

"Well that was lucky," Beth had said.

But it hadn't been. She had wanted to explain the custom, how wives weren't allowed to take their husbands' names, how women weren't considered important enough. A name meant everything in Korea, and only children were given their fathers' names. All a woman could do was pass on the honour.

The arch of her right foot went into spasm and she pointed her toe back to stretch it out. Her ankle joint popped. Her body was coming undone. Joints and limbs were seizing up, ready to fall apart like cheap furniture. Her skin was becoming one giant stretch mark and a rash had broken out on her thigh. She laid her head on the back of the tub. The air was heavy with steam and she lifted her belly to see the red line where her pale dry skin met the wet hot pink that had been underwater. She scooped water over her belly and let it cascade, then sank lower in the tub, submerging her head for an instant before pushing herself back up with her legs. Her jaw relaxed as she rubbed sweat and water off her face. She'd been clenching her teeth and she ran her tongue over them.

The baby still hadn't kicked.

She imagined the doctor's face, sheet white, as he explained to her what had gone wrong.

She dipped her head quickly beneath the water again. What if Joseph's death was spreading like a disease?

The hot water and steam felt suddenly claustrophobic and she wrapped the plug's chain around her toe and tugged it out. The air was still warm but she shivered as the water sank slowly away from her body, and she lifted herself back onto the porcelain edge, letting water slide off her skin and onto the tiled floor. She felt light-headed, as if all of her blood had gathered in her belly and left the rest of her empty.

Even if she lost the baby she'd still have to deliver it.

She stood up and grabbed the towel from the back of the door. She was being ridiculous. Of course she was. But still a tiny voice whispered: *You are carrying death.*

The River

The copper river is hidden from Deloume Road by a dense overhang of cedar, maple and alder boughs. For two and a half seasons the trickle-creep of water tugs at fern roots, saplings and skunk cabbage as it moves without breath.

The flow undercuts the bare banks in places so the edges of the river pass underground, and there isn't enough firm soil for trees to take root above. But trees a few feet up the banks spread their roots towards the stream, and some of these dangle through the soil and hang along the margins underwater. Small trout and crayfish swim among them, shadows darting through patches of sunlight.

In August and the Indian summer of early autumn the river slows, and its water gathers in shaded pools. Parts of the river dry up and expose smooth stones that are blue and black and dark grey when wet, but dry powder white and green.

The Jesus-feet of water striders dimple the surface of the large pool beneath Deloume's pipes. Leaves dry and fall onto this surface of sun-dusted glass, and these spade-shaped alder and father-hand maple leaves float for a time, gathering together to map out the otherwise imperceptible motion of current, and in their shadows crayfish emerge from beneath stones to search for food. New leaves fall, and the old leaves sink beneath the water and come to rest on stones and muddy silt. And this layer of murky leaf carpet reflects the kaleidoscope pattern of shifting sunlight through trees, and the water appears golden brown throughout, shades of honey and rust.

The pool smells of tree root and wet earth, and patches of swamp lantern give off a musky scent, their yellow flower husks bright even in shade. Clouds of river flies hover in unison, their tiny wings beating through the sunlight, ready to torment the deer that come to the river. The mule deer approach the pools slowly, pausing with lifted heads before bowing at the neck and leaning to drink, ears twitching all the while, eyes wide. Some are does with fawns following, their young bodies decorated with white spots like lichen-covered logs, their eyes too large for their narrow heads. The does watch while their young drink, and nudge them if they take too long.

Bucks are rare this close to the road, but when one does come, it carries an air of Shakespearean tragedy, of the right to a throne banished into wilderness. Their shoulders and hindquarters are thick with tight muscle, and their crown of bone branch never tangles in underbrush or knocks against trees. A fully grown buck's eyes are shaded by its antlers and appear less wide, as if more cunning and confident than the does'. When a buck stoops to drink, it doesn't bow, instead the whole forest and the river seem to tilt upwards.

The stretch of dry patches and pools reaches farther than the children of Deloume can walk or see, so the river doesn't begin or end. And the still pools draw the children to their treeless banks and cool water, to patches of light, the rainbow dance of trout scale and the wet colours of leaf bottom; and to their shadowy depths, unseen crayfish claws and faces staring up, eyes unblinking.

I kneel and stir the water with my fingers.

The shade beside the river is cool and sunlight in leaf-gap patterns plunges deep into the water, stretching to the silt, stones and dead leaves on the bottom.

"I bet that leaf hanging from the spider's web is gone now," I say.

A maple leaf falls from a branch, still green. It lands on the water face down, its veined back dry for a moment yet. I look at the back of my hand, at the blue vessels and rough skin. You lean over the edge, flicker and shadow, as if projected light before me. I watch you straining to see your reflection, but the maple leaf swirls slowly in front of you on the water's surface, blocking your view.

Blood sinking through water.

We wait for a moment together, beside the cedar-sap pool of trapped sunlight, the silence momentous, and then, slowly, you lift your small, pale hand and point to the deepest section of the pool.

ANDY

He leaned over the river and watched the compass swing from his neck, the reflection distorted as Matthew and Josh cast their fishing lines. Ripples.

"Careful Andy," said Matthew.

He crouched beside the river and clutched the compass to stop it from swinging.

Be careful. Wet.

"Forget it," said Josh. "There's nothing in here."

"Yeah, let's go," said Matthew. "Come on Andy. Let's see what Grandpa's doing."

The two older boys climbed up the bank to the stop sign and their bikes.

He reached out and touched the water, then licked his finger. It tasted like pennies. He pulled the shoelace over his head and let the compass dangle above the water, watching as it touched its own reflection and the two melted into each other.

"Andy!" yelled Matthew from the road.

He jerked his hand back and dropped the compass. It sank quickly in the shallow water, the shoelace floating above it. Seaweed. He looked around to see if his brother was watching. The two boys were invisible behind trees lining the road. He reached for the compass, touching the surface of the water, his fingers resting on it. Glass.

"Andy, we're leaving!"

Go.

He left the river and ran to catch up with his brother, his heart pounding and the older boy's voice ringing in his ears as he stumbled up the bank to Deloume.

THE BUTCHER

He stared without blinking at the door of the deli, the rectangle a blur. He squinted and the lines sharpened. He couldn't put off picking up his glasses much longer. At first he'd thought his eyes were just tired in the evenings. Nothing to worry about, he was probably just working too hard. But now the time of day didn't matter. He could read fine, but beyond nine or ten feet everything seemed to be slowly bleeding together. It was silly, but somehow the idea of actually wearing glasses felt like it would make the condition real.

Miles had slept in the shed again the night before, and for some reason he felt the urge to blame his problem on the boy. He chuckled. It was exactly what his father would have done. Leaned on some ridiculous superstition instead of trusting a doctor. The boy wasn't cursed, just hard done by, and that wasn't something that rubbed off on anyone else. Besides, the boy needed his help. That morning, when he'd checked the shed, he'd found the blanket folded and the floor swept.

Perhaps he should just admit defeat and go and pick up his prescription. It was a long walk without a car though, and it was getting late in the afternoon. Maybe if he planned ahead Sam could give him a lift.

He stepped out back and blinked at the blurring telephone wires along Deloume, trying to make up his mind.

"Sorry," said a voice behind him.

He turned and squinted, then realized it was Miles.

"I-I'm sorry," repeated Miles.

They stood in silence. Finally the butcher spoke. "For what?" he said, cringing at the throaty inflections of his own accent.

Miles's shoulders rose in a shrug.

"I believe you." He tried to focus on the boy's eyes, which he imagined were brown like his own son's. "Are you hungry?"

Miles nodded.

"Okay then, follow me," he said, leading the way inside the deli. He stumbled over a door jamb but recovered quickly, cursing under his breath in Ukrainian. He looked back at the boy. Miles hadn't moved. He tried to smile at him despite the pain in his toe. "Long day," he said.

He continued into the deli, this time walking gingerly, waving for Miles to follow. He pointed to a stool at the counter, then cut bread and ham.

The boy ate quickly in silence, wiping his hands on his shirt when he was finished.

"So, enough?"

Miles nodded again.

"Do your parents know where you sleep?" He hadn't meant to ask the question so abruptly, and they stared at each other, the words clustered on the counter between them.

That same shrug.

"What are you going to do in winter, when it's cold?"

Silence.

"Will you go home then?"

"No. I-I'm never going . . . I'm sorry," said Miles, sliding off the stool.

The butcher shook his head and smiled. "But you haven't done anything wrong."

The boy edged towards the door, but he pulled up another stool and sat down, gesturing for Miles to do the same.

"Don't worry about that yet," he said. "It's still summer."

Miles sat down again.

"So. I think it's your turn. You can ask me anything you want, and I promise to tell the truth."

It was almost a minute before Miles spoke. "Do you like pigs?" he asked.

"No," said the butcher, surprised by the speed of his own answer.

Another pause. And then Miles spoke again, this time his voice less timid. "Why are you squinting?"

He started to explain but stopped. "Maybe I'm getting old," he conceded. "Next question."

MILES FORD

He stood outside the deli and arranged his thoughts. Why was the butcher so nice to him? Did he want something?

He walked down the road until he reached the stop sign. He stooped to pick up a rock but paused. He needed to think. The butcher was right. It would start getting cold soon. Maybe he'd have to go home. His dad was gonna be even more angry than usual.

He climbed down to the river and sat in the shade. There was no breeze and the leaf shadows hung still. He tried not to move too much. Just look. Gliders gathered on the water, and bits of dust swirled above them. There were more water gliders than he'd first noticed. Ten, fifteen, their tiny feet dimpling the water's surface. A leaf floated across the pool.

The water wasn't still at all.

He sat down and tried not to breathe too quickly. Why hadn't he seen all this before? Maybe he had. Maybe he'd looked right at it all and just never really noticed. His thoughts began to settle. Birds on a telephone wire.

The butcher was alone a lot. Just like him. Sometimes customers came in but they weren't his friends. The customers' words were just for getting things. Not for really talking. Not like when Matthew and Josh talked. They talked for hours some-times, but they didn't want anything back, just more words.

Maybe he could talk to the butcher the same way. What would he say?

Do you still hate pigs?

Are you scared sometimes?

Those words weren't enough. He needed to remember the kinds of words the other boys used.

He stood and climbed into the metal pipe. At first all he could hear was the echo of his own breathing. Then the words came to him.

God. Bike. Brother. Home.

The words grew into sentences, Matthew's and Josh's voices clear in his head.

I'm going home.

Is your brother there?

I'm getting a new bike for my birthday.

There must be a God.

Miles opened his eyes and his thoughts scattered. He needed his own words. He imagined the butcher sitting at the counter of the deli. But words wouldn't come. Maybe it would be better to get the butcher a present. To show they were friends. His mind walked through the junkyard outside the white trailer. Hubcaps. Rusting refrigerators. Bags of old nails. None of it was good enough for the butcher. It was his parents' fault. All they had was a junkyard.

He closed his eyes and imagined it all being cleared away, all of the rusty metal, tires and cracked windshields. Everything being loaded onto a flatbed truck and carried off down Deloume, the trailer left empty. And the dog off its chain and chasing the truck down the road. Then what should have taken months he imagined happening all at once: Grass growing in around potholes, and blackberry vines creeping over the rust-stained ground. Beetles and pill bugs crawling over roots, and ferns springing up along the sides of the trailer. A blue jay on the trailer's roof and a wasps' nest growing in paper strips, forming an oval under the eaves. A spider's web spreading in a snowflake pattern in one of the trailer's open windows.

He climbed out of the pipe, tears forming in the corners of his eyes. He blinked them out, warm and fast down his cheeks onto his jaw. He wiped them off with his sleeve.

He stood on the egg-shaped stones beside the river. His eyes followed them to the edge of the water and stopped. A shoelace floated up from something metal. He grabbed the shoelace and pulled it out of the river. A locket dangled from the end. He fiddled with the slippery disc and it popped open. A compass. His dad used to have one just like it. He'd shown it to him when he was little. Said it was his grandpa's. Miles snapped shut the lid and polished the metal surface on his shirt like an apple. The initials G.D. were carved into the metal.

Who had left it there? He looked back at the shadowy mouth of the pipe that passed beneath the road. Maybe he could give it to the butcher as a present. But what if the compass was just another piece of junk, more garbage like at home? What if the butcher hated it?

Two crows landed in the branches of a tree above him, squawking and provoking each other until they locked talons and beaks in a blur of flapping black wings and tumbled from the tree, each taking flight inches before hitting the water. He stayed still for a moment after the commotion, watching a lone black feather turn slowly on the water's surface.

July, 1899

Two blankets for settlement land. That's what they said it cost back in '62 for those who'd come on the HMS *Hecate* into Cowichan Bay and then south along the island's east coast to the mill. Two blankets to the Natives for acres of forest. For countless miles of lumber. The land had cost more now, but not much. Not land that had already been logged once. Its masts taken. Not land too far from the sawmill to amount to anything, land this lonely and dense, its logging trails already forgotten. So he'd spent nearly every penny he had on it—staked his claim on the promised land and hired men from the mill to clear the old trail properly. Men used to hard work. Ford, Smith, Toews, McNabb. And he'd promised them better payment for their labours.

Overheard voices whispering to him.

Why the devil anyone'd clear an old logging trail I don't know.

Shut yours Toews. He's payin'.

He rolled sap between his fingers and breathed in, trying to memorize the scent. The Morse code of Brag, and Scavenger folding its wings into its black coat, its hand-in-pocket walk. Mapmaker circled, the hook-beaked god looking down on his trail through the wilderness.

He'd quit work with the Royal Geological Society to come back. To stay. They'd tried to talk him out of it of course.

You're a surveyor Deloume. Keep it together.

Limestone nearby. Could quarry it.

They all thought he was mad. Back in England. Here. Even the men he'd hired. If only they could see the place as he did.

Falling moths. A sign. His land. From the Douglas fir to the river, where he stood, the water slower now, the spring runoff finished. Clear to the bottom. The stumble-lap of the current, the slow spin of leaves, gentle flow pulling at the banks, at the rooted mud, soil and stones. He knelt and touched the water, the shock snapping at his fingertips. Impossible to tell if it was ice-cold or burning hot. His own reflection then, distorted. Thick beard. Sunken eyes. He raised his hand to his face and ran his fingers across his forehead, the water running down his skin in thin, icy lines. Another face in the water, pale and small, staring up at him, eyes wide. Then gone.

What did the river hold in its ageless memory? And what could it know? He was dust to dust, ash. But the river was everything he wasn't, and everything it held shifted and changed. He was a narrative of bones from clay, and the river was life without breath, stolen images.

"River, your name is Secret."

AVRIL

S he put one lasagna in the middle of the table, the glass dish hot even through oven mitts.

"Thanks Mom," said Matthew. He held a wooden elastic gun in one hand. It had clothespins for hammers.

Andy sat across from him holding a shorter weapon by the nozzle.

"Aw, come on now boy. It's wrong way up," said her father.

"Don't even start," she said, taking a second lasagna out of the oven and placing it on the counter to cool. "Of all the things you could have brought for them." She glanced at Matthew. "Put those away!" Her voice came out sharper than she'd intended, and her embarrassment made her even more upset. "If your father were home you'd be heading to your room with an empty stomach." But it wasn't true. And deep down she was glad her dad had brought them gifts. No way she was going to admit it though.

"Looks like they're going over even better than the potato guns I brought a couple years ago," he said, winking at her. "Hell, they're boys after all."

"You watch your language, Dad. I don't want them picking anything up from that mouth of yours."

Her father laughed, phlegm catching in his throat. "Better

holster those for dinner boys," he said, nodding at Matthew and Andy's weapons.

Matthew took both guns and slipped them under his chair as she dished out the lasagna and sat down.

"Say, how come that other dish is on the counter? You holdin' out on us?" asked her dad.

"It's for Irene Choi up the road," she said.

"Her husband got shot," said Matthew.

"Choi, eh? She a Chink or something?"

"Dad! And no, she's Korean."

"A gook then."

"That's enough!" she said.

Silence around the table. Her father's face twisted into a wry smile.

"What's a gook?" asked Matthew.

Silence again.

"It's a mean thing to call someone," she said.

"Oh," said Matthew, looking down at his plate. "Is Mr. Henry a gook?"

She sighed and looked at her dad. He stared back. He seemed to be trying not to laugh.

"No," she said. "Al's Native."

"Native? You all livin' on a reserve now or something?"

"That's it. I can't handle this." She pushed back her chair and stood up. Her boys stared at her and she felt her face burn red. She glared at her father, angry at herself for letting him get her so worked up.

"Okay, everyone just relax." Her dad stood and picked up his hat from the back of the chair. "Could use a smoke anyhow." He walked out of the kitchen.

Avril swallowed hard and tried not to pay attention to the eyes of her children.

"Gook," said Andy, sticking his fork into his lasagna.

JONAH DAVIES

He stood outside and stared at his truck. It'd be easy to go. David was home from work, and he could hear him trying to calm Avril down inside. Finally the door opened behind him and David walked over.

Neither of them spoke for a moment.

"Guess I'm supposed to apologize now," he said finally. He looked down at the hat in his hands and ran a finger around the stiff brim.

"Mmmm," said David.

"Can't teach an old dog, I guess."

Quiet again. The sky's blue just starting to fade.

"Nice truck," said David.

"Yeah, she's a beaut."

"Expensive?"

"Naw. Bought her from a friend. Gave me a deal."

A dog barked next door.

"I haven't seen Avril this wound up since—"

"The funeral," Jonah finished.

David nodded. "Will you stay long?"

"Just a couple days. If that's all right."

"Of course it is."

The two men made eye contact briefly and Jonah chuckled.

"I was hoping to head south to Arizona after. Got a friend down there. Been promising to visit for years."

"You know she's glad you're here, right?"

Another silence. He felt David's hand on his shoulder, just a quick pat, then his son-in-law was gone.

He picked up his pipe from the windowsill where he'd left it and tapped it on the side of the house. A glob of wet ash fell from the pipe onto the ground. He tilted it again and a few drops of discoloured water dribbled out. He looked at the windowsill. Bone-dry. Damn it all, what a mess.

He heard a shuffle behind him and glanced over his shoulder. Matthew stood in the doorway.

"Know anything about this?" he asked, waving the pipe at the boy.

Matthew hesitated. "Mom . . . Mom said it'd kill you."

"So what? So you filled it with water?"

Matthew nodded. The boy looked on the verge of tears. Jonah put his pipe back on the windowsill and sighed.

"Come here kid," he said.

Matthew walked over to him slowly, looking down at his feet.

"You shouldn't have done it."

Matthew nodded.

"But your mom's right. It probably will kill me."

Matthew looked up, startled.

"I tell you what—we'll make a deal. I'll try not to smoke it so much if you'll promise not to talk like me. Not ever."

Matthew looked confused but he shrugged his shoulders. "Okay," he said. "Deal."

They shook hands, the boy's skin smooth and soft. Strong grip though. Matthew walked back to the door and slipped past Avril, who stood with her arms crossed. How long had she been there?

He'd been wrong about her. She didn't look the way he'd remembered. There were more lines on her face and traces of grey through her auburn hair. Just like her mother's.

AL HENRY

They still hadn't found the wreck of the plane. Three days now. He wasn't sure he could fully believe it yet. Everything about it seemed strange, as if he were detached from reality, watching his own life unfold on television, or reading about himself in a book. He closed his eyes and tried to re-create the crash again, and this time saw it happen on Deloume Road, saw the plane's wing flaps adjusting in tilts, its landing gear dropping and smoke billowing from behind the Otter's single propeller. The trees were too close to the sides of the road in places, but the wheels touched down for an instant and bounced. A wing caught a tree trunk, the metal screaming and shearing through bark, the plane spinning off the road and cartwheeling into the forest.

He walked the tire marks on Deloume until he came to pieces of wing embedded in a cedar trunk, as if they were a part of the tree that had been revealed when the collision tore off its bark. The air was cold and the metal shone in the sun.

He followed the trail of uprooted broom and flattened grass. Ahead of him the plane lay sideways against a pair of thick maples. The earth leading to the plane was ploughed, pieces of landing gear, shredded tire, wire and glass scattered through the woods.

No dogs barked. The birds were silent. The hum of insects was gone, and the air was full of smoke and the smell of burning plastic. A hose leaked. Metal contracted, bent under pressure, expanded in the heat of friction in hollow thumps and crunches. He stood before the hulking wreck and stared with watering eyes at a massive crow that had landed on top of it. The bird cocked its head and stared back at him.

"Get away from my son," he said, taking a step forward. "You can't fucking have him!"

The crow turned its head and looked at him with its other eye. Al's skin goosebumped and he breathed out a cloud of cold air and smoke. The crow spread its wings and lifted off, its flapping like the sound of sheet metal vibrating in the wind. The bird circled over him and blocked the sun. Then it was gone.

In the roots of a tree beside the plane lay the body of his son's co-pilot, his neck bent sideways and backwards. He was still partially buckled into his seat, which had been ripped out of the aircraft and lay beside him. The man's eyes were open, staring up at the leaves that moved silently in the breeze. The body had disrupted a line of ants, and now the march continued over the still pilot, black and red dots finding their way over the twisted corpse to rejoin the line.

He stepped over the body to the other side of the plane. He looked inside the broken mess of the cockpit. His son's body was still strapped in, his head hanging forward, hidden behind his long hair. The door was open on one hinge, and his son's arm dangled out of the plane. Al hesitated. He put his hand on his son's shoulder and tried to turn the body but the seat belts held him fast.

Al tried to breathe deeply but his lungs only took in a gasp and his pulse throbbed at his temples. Slowly, he cradled his son's head in his hands and turned it to face him.

Al's eyelids snapped open and he saw Beth watching him from the doorway.

"You yelled something," she said, teetering on the threshold of the room.

"I saw it," said Al.

She was watching him silently, biting her bottom lip.

"Jesus, I was there. I saw his plane go down. He's not . . ." Al paused as tears formed in the corners of his wife's eyes. "Beth, he wasn't dead."

IRENE

How long had it been? She'd woken from a nap, startled by what she thought was a kick, and had sat for hours waiting for another. But had she felt any? She couldn't remember. In and out of sleep. Had she dozed off and missed them?

She finished her cup of mint tea and went to the washroom yet again before returning to the living room. Beth had been over again earlier that day and had tried to help her stay calm.

"Don't worry," she'd said. "You're probably just so used to the kicks and bumps that you're not noticing them any more." And she'd told her to be patient, to try to think of something, anything, else. But that was so much easier said than done. The thought of having Joseph's child without him had haunted her for months, but now losing that same child had her mind racing from one fear to the next.

On the coffee table sat a stack of letters, twelve of them, that Joseph had sent her before it had happened. One of them had arrived after she'd been given the news and it had taken her days to find the courage to open it. She'd memorized nearly every word, reading them out loud over and over, practising each syllable, as if by learning the language well she might cast some spell to bring him back.

On the front of the top envelope she traced her finger over

her name, written in English. The characters still seemed random to her, strange, without any logic or order. They were not so much fitted together as lined up like schoolchildren during a fire drill.

She wrote her name in Hangul with her finger on the envelope. The Korean language fit together so well, built symbol upon symbol, perfectly phonetic, perfectly logical. And the pieces had meaning too. Perhaps that was what really made English so foreign, how the letters meant nothing alone, or at least nothing more than a short sound. How could anything meaningful ever come from such a haphazard foundation? It was like trying to toss bricks into the shape of a house. The lines of Hangul though, so different, so full of intention. Three shapes: a circle, for sky or god; a vertical line, for people; and a horizontal line, for the earth. So writing unified people with god, and people with the earth, and all three were present in each word. There was a wholeness to the language, a feeling of completion and unity.

And yet, somehow it didn't excite her the way English did. Korean was easier to speak but its confines made her feel claustrophobic. It was so imposing with its hierarchies and six levels of politeness, in how it seemed poetic, but was also clinical, perhaps lacking something. Could it be joy? English was ridiculous, there was no doubt; it made no sense, following rules only occasionally, but it also allowed room to move, a freedom of expression and wordplay that was dominated only by loose structure and motivated by communication, not grammar.

She had so wanted her child to learn English from a young age, become fluent, so that the words that eluded and frustrated her would be second nature to her child. She tried to imagine those words infused into a person. What would that look like? How different would her child be from her? How like Joseph?

Please kick.

A knock at her front door. She looked towards the sound, startled, unsure about whether to answer it. She brushed her hair out of her face, retied the elastic holding the ponytail and walked to the door. In Korea she would have hidden in the bathroom until her makeup was on and her hair was styled properly, pregnant or not.

She opened the door and looked at Al without speaking, the greetings of two languages colliding and leaving her tongue-tied.

"Hi," said Al. "Uh, Beth mentioned you hadn't been able to hang that painting . . . the one I . . ."

They stood awkwardly as her mind raced through the house to the painting of her husband that still leaned against the wall on the living room floor.

"Unless . . ." he continued, scratching his head and looking everywhere but into her eyes. "Unless you don't want . . ." Again his voice trailed off, and she glanced down at the small orange tool box he carried.

"Thank you," she said finally, relieved to hear her own voice.

She opened the door wider and motioned for him to come in, pointing towards the living room.

They stood side by side in front of the painting, and for another moment she couldn't find the words.

"I don't know how to say," she mumbled, surprising herself by touching his shoulder.

Al looked her in the eyes, as if trying to read meaning in them. She felt tears well up and she smiled to show him that she appreciated his painting, trying to form another sentence but in the end only managing one word. "Gift."

He looked away. "Seemed like you should have it," he said softly. "It might need a proper frame, but maybe we could just put it up like this now, hang it from the canvas frame instead. Sometimes paintings look better without borders anyways."

She wiped her eyes. She could understand nearly everything he said, although she wasn't exactly sure what a "frame" was.

She was too nervous to ask him about his son. Afraid to hear his answer. He interrupted her thoughts with a question of his own.

"So, where should we put it?"

She pointed to a patch of bare wall near the rocking chair and watched as he held up the painting, looking to her for approval. She nodded and he marked spots on the wall with a pencil. He hung the painting with such care, small nails in his mouth as he measured and hammered. Such focus.

Why was he doing this for her? He could have painted anyone.

She practised the question in her head while he worked, waiting until he was finished. At last she said it.

"Why did you paint Joseph?"

She watched his forehead wrinkle. He looked at the portrait on the wall and then shook his head.

"I'm not exactly sure," he said, putting his tool box on the coffee table.

She followed his eyes to the envelopes and saw him read the name of the sender, then try to hide his reaction.

"I guess I just couldn't get his face out of my head."

He spoke haltingly, as if worried he might choose the wrong word. Just like her. He stepped back beside her and they both looked at the portrait in its new place.

"I'm sorry he's . . ." said Al, catching himself.

"Not coming home," she finished.

He nodded. "It's the first portrait I've done for years. First one I finished at least."

Airplanes to portraits. Irene thought about it for a moment in the growing quiet. "Sky to people," she said, finding each word and pronouncing them slowly.

"Yeah, I guess," said Al. "I never really thought about it like that though."

He kept talking and Irene shifted from one foot to the other, her eyes never leaving the face of Joseph as she listened to the sound of Al's voice, the way each word left his throat and mouth and then hung in the air around them.

BETH

She sat in the car on the driveway wiping her eyes and try-ing to collect her thoughts. The key was already in the ignition but she didn't turn it. It was impossible not to worry about Al. This dream of his. He seemed so sure all of a sudden that Carson was going to be all right. But why? His hope was mistimed. For the first couple of days after the phone call he'd acted like Carson was dead, but now, just when he needed to accept the fact that his son was lost, he was hopeful again.

A fly droned along the dashboard, crashing into the wind-screen again and again. She rolled down the window and tried to shoo it outside but it just kept buzzing into the glass. She gave up and slumped back in the seat.

She'd called a friend in Vancouver, a psychiatrist, and her advice had been simple: encourage him to *do* something. So Beth had sent him back to Irene's to hang the portrait. A strange request maybe, but at least it would get him out of the house and into some fresh air for a bit. And he'd have to talk to Irene. It'd be good for both of them.

It had been difficult to see Al so sad, but this was worse, this false hope. Not that she didn't want him to be right. Anything was possible of course. But ... She gripped the steering wheel, the veins on her hands bulging greenish blue between her knuckles.

Then there was Irene, panicking that her baby wasn't moving. And after Beth had felt it kick just the other day. She'd told Irene to start writing down the number of kicks she felt so that she didn't have to rely on her tired mind to remember each one. Still, it was worth making a doctor's appointment. If only to calm Irene. In her experience pregnant women were usually wrong about things like this. They were stressed and exhausted by the pregnancy and whatever else was going on. And Irene's case was extreme. The girl had so much to think about.

Beth twisted the key in the ignition and the car's engine turned over. A quick trip to the grocery store in Mill Bay. She'd pick up a few things for Irene too. She checked her mirrors but couldn't quite focus on the glass.

God, what if Irene was right?

AVRIL

She watched her father through the sliding glass door. He sat on the deck in a lawn chair smoking his pipe, the grey haze floating over the backyard. The evening was cool and clouds were building into a front.

She opened the door and pulled a chair over to her father. "Mind if I join you?"

"Your house," he said, smiling as he exhaled smoke.

She sat down, the fabric seat of the lawn chair noisy against its metal frame.

"Want me to put this out?" he asked, wiggling the pipe in his mouth.

She shook her head.

"Good. Took me long enough to get it going again."

The day's heat seemed to be riding out on the breeze and the setting sun turned the towering clouds pink and orange on the horizon. She breathed in a waft of tobacco, its flavours mixing sweetly with pollen in the air. The wooden planks of the deck were still warm from the sun and she curled her toes beneath her feet.

"Dad . . . you don't have to leave soon, okay?"

He blew out a smoke ring and chuckled. "See that? Harder than it looks."

"Dad?"

"Okay, okay. I heard ya."

"It's just that I . . . the boys like having you around so much . . ."

They sat quietly before her dad spoke again. "It should've been me. I know you're thinking it too."

"No, Dad, I —"

"Don't matter. You ain't wrong."

Silence again.

"God, I miss her like hell."

"I . . . I know you do, Dad."

Her father brushed her arm and found her hand, his fingers and palm warm from the pipe. A few drops of rain hit the wooden planks around them, tapping out a warning, but neither of them moved as the clouds overhead turned dark and the horizon faded to embers.

SAM TOEWS

The road had gone quiet and he leaned against the door frame, waiting for his ears to adjust to the smaller sounds of the dark. The sliver moon hung as if frail, and didn't give off much light.

More room for the stars, he thought, as he traced Orion's Belt. Clouds were massing over Mount Baldy and drops of rain blew in on the breeze.

A truck moved slowly up the road, its headlights like yellow eyes scanning the gravel. It was Bob's truck, going maybe ten miles an hour.

Shit. Bob was out looking for Miles.

When the truck had passed out of sight he went into his house and closed and locked the door. The house was still. Not like when he'd been a kid. His parents and grandparents in the other bedrooms. Even the air wasn't right now. Stale. Unstirred. He climbed the stairs, undressed and washed his face before getting into bed. Even though the double bed was half empty he stayed on one side, lying on his back, listening to the faint rumble of the truck's engine as it passed by again, still slow, still idling unsteadily, like a bull pawing at the dirt, snorting before the gate opens.

Rain

Rain hits the dusty road quietly at first, then builds momentum, falling faster until its percussion covers up all the other noises, pulling down scents. All at once it stops. The dark road smells of wet dust. Colours shift and spread in the torn-canvas sunset. Violet and red.

My arms goosebump. I lean against the stop sign and listen to the slow creep of the river. The road is quieting down now. A solitary dog barks. Crickets. The rustle of birds to nest, owl stretch.

I can see it all happening along the road. An artist leans out of his studio window and wonders how he missed July. A farmer locks a gate and stops to look at a sow lying in a stall. The pig winks. A woman feels her swollen womb and realizes that the windows of her house are closed, and have been for days. She pushes them open, letting the rain-washed air fill her home. A boy putting on his pyjamas remembers spelling tests and the itch of socks. His mother watches him from the doorway.

The smell of wet lawn clippings. Beads of dark water along a windowsill, in a pothole, on cedar boughs and gravel, fence posts and mailboxes. The trampled grass and bent ferns are wet now, and smell sweet.

There are white moths over the road, brave despite the rain, and we walk away from the stop sign up Deloume towards the driveways, the sound of the river fading. The floral sky sinks behind evergreen hills and the darkening moonscape of Mount Baldy. We pause at old Bob Ford's driveway, and I wonder what you think of the place now. A caged light bulb hangs from a nail in a telephone pole beside the road, lighting up the entrance to the junkyard. It flickers on and off, powered by some ancient generator humming out of sight.

A brush of bat wings on air and a moth disappears in shadow. The purple night is turning to ash, the grey closing in around us, and my arms goosebump again. A daddy-long-legs flirts with the bulb, its limbs impossibly long for such thin wings. We stand in silence until the flickering light and brush of insects against the cage become unbearable and I clear my throat.

"I need you to understand," I say again, trying to find words that match my guilt. "It just happened."

In the water. Face down.

Owl-hoot from the trees around us. Moths congregate around the light, their wings casting moving shadows on the ground at my feet. A drop of rain hits my ear.

A car rolls past with its headlights on, slowing as it passes the light. The front windows are down and the windshield wipers remain still. A woman's head leans against the driver's shoulder. The driver's left arm is out the window and I imagine drops of rain freckling his skin. In the back seats two children lean their heads against the windows, trying to use rolled-up beach towels as pillows. They are sapped from the disappeared afternoon sun and barely conscious of the slow drive home. An inner tube is fastened to the roof of the car with bungee cords.

The car slows again farther up the road as a fawn stumbles across Deloume, disappearing into living shadows. And as the car turns up a driveway and the engine is cut, the sound of rain begins again.

I try to look you in the eyes, but you're too far outside the border of light. I shiver in the breeze as rain falls around us drop by drop. Slowly. Nightfall is complete now, and outside the ring of light it's too dark to see.

MATTHEW

Drops of rain slid down his bedroom window. His breath fogged the glass and he moved his head back so he could see out again. The sky was sooty, overcast. It had been raining all night and everything had been knocked out of the air. All the greens were darker, the colour of steamed broccoli.

He wandered downstairs past his mother reading in the living room and down again to the basement. His grandpa was taking a nap upstairs and Andy was at a doctor's appointment with their father. Matthew wondered if his brother had left the compass in the house or taken it with him. He'd better not have lost it. Andy was always the same with his things: first he'd cling to something day and night, then he'd hide it around the house until finally he forgot about it altogether. He checked the pockets of one of Andy's coats and looked beneath the cushions of the old Hide-A-Bed. Nothing. Where else? There was a half-made Lego castle in the corner of the rec room and he got down on his hands and knees to peer inside the lone tower. A brown pine cone. How long ago had Andy put it there? How long ago had he forgotten about it?

He snapped a piece of Lego into place on top of the castle then looked around the room at the scattered toys: Matchbox cars, Star Wars figurines, a plastic sword and his new wooden elastic gun with clothespin triggers. He set up a row of tiny army men, German infantry in grey moulded plastic, and shot elastic bands at them until only one was left standing.

"Go and tell Adolf what happened. I dare you."

He shot another elastic band over the lone infantryman's head to make him run faster.

Rain in the summer was almost too much to bear and he felt a tingle in his feet and limbs, an itching to be outside on his bike or climbing a tree.

On the rec room wall hung a painting of an airplane, a red water bomber diving towards a lake with its water catch opening. He stared at the painting and wondered why it made him uneasy. He'd seen it thousands of times. He touched the oil surface and felt the texture of the paint. He wanted it to happen. He wanted the bomber to pick up water and drop it on a forest fire that raged out of control, threatening to spread along Deloume Road, burning the stop sign and the fences, the barns and blackberry bushes. The fire would dry up the river and then devour the houses. Only the water bomber stood in the way of calamity. And there would be more planes, and each would drop load after load of water until the fire was nothing more than a few singed cedars and curling black ferns. But the painting looked as though it didn't want him to think these things, as if he should look at it and imagine a world where nothing moved, like in the rec room, with its double-paned windows and dusty carpet.

He stood on his tiptoes and opened one of the basement windows, heard the steady beat of rain on the roof and driveway, felt the cool air, clean now, shot through with scents of wet grass and trees. Faint bird chirps sank from a swallow's nest in

the eaves far above the window. A gust of wind blew rain sideways into his face and he blinked drops from his eyelashes.

His father's blue Toyota Corona rolled up the driveway and
parked, and his brother got out and ran for the door. Matthew
closed the window and glanced once more at the painting.
Everything moves, he thought, as his brother opened the door
behind him.

JOSH

He sat alone in his parents' living room. The empty couch and chairs around him seemed hushed, as if waiting for him to leave so they could talk, and their silence turned into a white noise in his ears. His mom had locked herself in the bedroom earlier that morning after a fight with his dad, but he couldn't hear her crying any more. And his dad had stormed out and driven off somewhere.

"Rain shmain," he said finally, his voice louder than he'd intended. He'd already checked the TV. There was nothing on but soap operas. He'd tried to watch one but it was just more grown-ups arguing.

He looked at his reflection in the china cabinet window, then at the ornately carved dark wood and the dust on it. The vacuum cleaner sat on the floor, its cord plugged into a socket down the hall out of sight. He pressed the power button on the vacuum with his foot to kill the silence again, the hose slithering to life. He clicked it off the same way. The motor rattled as it stopped.

A checkerboard sat on the coffee table, the game finished, and he tried to remember if he'd won or lost. Both, he thought, and he looked up at the wall where a painting of an airplane hung in a thick gold frame. He remembered asking his dad if it was real gold and his dad had laughed, told him he was being silly. He should have known better. The painting was of a small white plane with skis landing on water, only it hadn't quite touched down. Or was it taking off? He didn't think so but he wasn't sure, and he let his eyes relax, the picture blurring into colours and haze. No matter how long he looked at it, it would never change. The plane would never take off or land.

What good was that?

He stood up and found his shoes and jacket. He left the door unlocked and went outside, picking up his bike and drying off the seat with his sleeve. Rain beaded on his jacket and ran down his arms to his hands. He pulled up his hood and pedalled down the driveway.

Rain soaked the Scotch broom and drops clung to tent caterpillars' nests in the alders, the cocoons sagging under the extra weight. His bike tires sounded like they were sucking on the tarred gravel, and water spun up into his legs and backwards in a rooster tail. He braced himself and sliced through a pothole. The impact shook the bike frame and he felt the familiar shock in his cold fingers and wrists. Water sprayed on each side of him. He passed driveways and took his time, circling back and around the puddles, trying to avoid the earthworms sprawled on the road like discarded chewing gum. He was nearly soaked through, and he could smell his wet blue jeans and jacket, his sweat mixing with rain. The air wasn't cold but it was sharper than it had been in months, and squeaky clean.

There weren't any cars or dogs ahead of him. The road was his. He left Matthew's, the Henrys' and the Fords' driveways behind him and passed the stop sign, its red paint wet and shiny. He did a double take and skidded to a stop, puzzling over the new holes in the sign, before riding on.

Beside the road cows congregated beneath broad-leaved branches, their tails keeping time with his legs. He whistled as he pedalled beside the pig farm, the sound sharp at first then spluttering out in the rain. He pushed hard up the steep hill, not stopping until he reached the top, where Deloume intersected with Shawnigan Mill Bay Road. A truck passed by on asphalt, then a car, then another. He looked back down Deloume, wondering what his mother would say if he kept going. The wide road stretched out before him. He'd been on it a million times in a car, but it wasn't the same as riding his bike on it. Being alone on it. He wasn't allowed to leave Deloume though, and if his mom found out she'd melt his bike down for scrap metal.

He turned his bike around and headed back down Deloume, gaining speed, swerving slightly to miss the big potholes, and then over the small jump at the bottom, his tires airborne for a second. He hit his brake and skidded, his tires sliding on the wet gravel and slowing to a stop. He pushed off his hood and let the rain soak his hair. A trickle of cold water crept down from his scalp onto his neck. His legs were tired now and he walked his bike to the stop sign.

Miles Ford emerged from the river onto the side of the road. The boy was soaked too. Miles looked at him and then at his bike.

"Hey," said Josh, realizing it was the first time he'd spoken to Miles for what seemed like years, although he must've seen him a hundred times that summer alone.

"Hey," said Miles back.

"You're wet," Josh mumbled, the awkwardness making him wish he hadn't stopped.

Miles didn't respond for a moment. Then he pointed at Josh's bike. "That yours?"

Josh nodded, and then he saw it hanging around Miles's neck from a shoelace. The compass.

Miles followed his gaze and the boy clutched the metal locket and held it against his chest, the two of them staring at each other in silence as rain fell in sheets.

ANDY

His brother's mouth moved and the words became fern spears hurtling towards him. He ducked and shuffled sideways along the wall. At his feet plastic army men lay slaughtered around a Lego castle. His brother's face was turning red now and he watched Matthew's lips and teeth and tongue pronounce a word.

"Compass."

Again, this time a hiss.

Andy covered his ears and sat down beside the castle. He peered inside. The pine cone was still there.

Safe.

His brother's hand gripped his shoulder and squeezed, not hard enough to hurt, but he couldn't ignore it.

He looked at his brother's mouth again.

"Where did you hide it Andy? Where is it?"

Andy looked at the pine cone and bit his lip.

Footsteps on carpet, the shuffle of slippers, and his father's feet appeared in the doorway. A deep voice.

". . . everything okay?"

Then Matthew's voice, higher pitched. "Yep. We're playing."

"Andy, son, are you listening?"

He nodded, imagining the carpet flat beneath his dad's brown slippers.

"Are you playing?" came his dad's voice again. The muscles in Andy's neck relaxed and he let his shoulders slump forward.

"Safe," said Andy. He watched his dad's slippers leave the room, the carpet springing up behind him, erasing his footprints.

He picked up an elastic band and tasted it. Burnt rubber. He looked quickly at Matthew's face. His brother stared at him. Andy looked down at the Lego again.

Yellow. Green. Blue. Red. Black. White. Grey.

"Seven," he said.

"I wish you'd look me in the eyes for once," said Matthew.

Andy could feel his brother staring at him still. His neck muscles tensed again, and he spat the elastic band into his hand. Tooth marks in the blue rubber.

"Did you hide it?"

Andy glanced at the pine cone again and this time let himself smile.

His brother followed his gaze and bent down and picked up the pine cone. Andy reached out for it but his brother lifted it above his head.

"I'll give it back when you tell me where the compass is," said Matthew.

Andy stood up, his chest tight. He tried to grab the pine cone but his brother stepped back.

"I," said Andy, his eyes never leaving the pine cone.

"Yes, you," said Matthew. "You can have it when you show me the compass."

Andy lunged forward, both hands outstretched, but his

foot caught the Lego castle, sending pieces across the room. His big toe throbbed and he sat down, holding it, his eyes on a tiny piece of Lego.

"Red," he said.

"This is useless," said Matthew. "I don't know why I even bother."

Matthew's hand closed around the pine cone and it crumbled, pieces falling to the carpet like ash, spreading out over the Lego.

Andy wailed once and tears blurred his vision. He bit the sleeve of his sweatshirt and rocked where he sat.

Tones from his brother into two words. ". . . your fault."

Andy covered his ears and focused on the motion of his body. His eyes cleared. The Lego was spread out over the floor. He counted the colours.

Grey socks shuffled on the carpet as his brother left. Pieces of pine cone lay scattered over the colours.

"Safe," he said, his eyes blurring again.

And then his chest began to relax and he stopped rocking, counted the colours again, checked for footprints.

His brother's socks walked back into the room and Matthew sat down directly in front of him.

Andy watched his mouth move.

"Sorry," said his brother's lips, making a round hole.

"Sorry," said Andy.

"No, I mean, I'm . . . you didn't . . ."

"Sorry," said Andy.

"Okay, okay, look at this."

Matthew held up a limp green shoelace and tied the ends together. Andy grabbed one end and put it in his mouth. Dusty.

He spat it out. Matthew put the shoelace around Andy's neck. He remembered the other shoelace and the shiny metal of the compass, the needle pointing at his parents.

"North," said Andy, watching his brother's lips break into a smile, his front teeth big and turned-in.

"Yeah," said Matthew, his throat vibrating as he talked. "North. You remember where it is now?"

Andy stood and walked out of the rec room to the door. The carpet pressed down beneath his socks. He looked behind him. Still no footprints. He walked to the side entrance of the house and pulled on his Velcro shoes.

He stood in the open door and let the sounds fill his head. Bird chirps from above him and raindrops on leaves and the driveway.

Pressure on his back from his brother's hand. A dog barked. The air was cool on his ears and his cheeks, and the corners of his eyes were tight from tears.

Tones from his brother's throat behind him but no words through the rhythm of rain falling. Then the rain stopped.

"North," he said, and stepped outside.

SAM TOEWS

He parked his pickup next to a pile of tires and hopped out of the cab. What a mess. As usual. Heaps of metal and old cars collecting rust. Looked like most of it had just fallen out of the grey sky. Paint peeled from a stack of car doors, colouring the weeds at his feet with flecks of blue and red. Lord knew how Bob lived there. Never mind a wife and kids. No wonder the eldest two had already left for good.

The trailer door opened and a short woman with thick arms emerged. She stared at him without smiling, dark circles beneath her eyes. Her white tank top was stained yellow and her dishwater hair cropped short. Bob's wife, Lisa. God, she looked something awful. He barely recognized her. It'd been six months at least since they'd spoken. Not that he'd had any reason to.

"Bob around?" he asked.

Lisa looked at his truck then back at him. "You here to buy something?" she asked, her thin lips oddly pale.

"Hope so," he answered. "I see you've cut your hair since . . ."

The woman leaned back inside the trailer and yelled for her husband. Sam ground his molars. He'd been up half the night thinking about whether or not to talk to them about Miles, hoping maybe he could smooth things over. Help the butcher a little. Now he wasn't so sure.

Bob brushed past his wife, buttoning a plaid jacket over a white undershirt and tightening the belt on his blue jeans as he walked. The man stopped a few feet from him. Sam forced a smile.

"How's things, Bob?"

Bob smiled, his teeth stained wooden. "You trying to sweeten the deal before we even get started?" he asked, chuckling and coughing.

"Naw. But it's been a good while. Plus I gotta do something to bring down your prices, don't I?"

Bob seemed to like that one and he laughed and again it turned into a cough. "Whatcha looking for?"

Sam glanced around the yard. The Doberman on its long chain stared at him. Damn dog made him nervous. It was too quiet.

"Need some chicken wire to fix up a garden fence is all. Not much though. Got any?" Sam spoke quickly.

"Yep," said Bob, turning and waving for him to follow. "Picked some up the other day."

They walked without speaking through the junkyard. Sam looked over his shoulder to see if the dog was following. It wasn't. For some reason that bothered him too. Everything about the place was off. Every pile crooked. It was the type of place where things rusted in the sun. Bob stopped beside a roll of wire fencing and nodded at it.

"This do?"

"Looks fine," said Sam, turning it over on the ground to check for rust. It was in good shape.

Bob put his hands on his hips and ran his tongue over his teeth, mouth closed, lips bulging. "You wanna make me an offer?" he asked, the side of his mouth curling.

"Sure. You want money or milk?"

The question seemed to catch the man off guard. He'd been expecting money. Years back a trade between the Toews and Fords would've been a given. Back before things went south between him and Bob.

"How much milk?"

"I don't know. Say twenty pints? Over a couple of months so it's fresh?"

Bob chewed his lip and bobbed his head while he thought about it. "Fencing's in pretty good shape," he said finally. "How about thirty?"

Sam smiled. Milk wasn't hard to come by. But he had principles. Plus Bob would skin him alive next time he needed something if he didn't barter some. Not like it was the first time he'd had to stand up to the man. His pulse quickened just thinking about it. The way Bob used to taunt him when they'd worked together on the farm. Calling him a hick. Telling him he'd never amount to nothing if he stayed there, that farming was a thing of the past. It'd come to blows once. Sam had got the worst of it and things had never quite been the same since. Hell, how many decades ago was that now?

"Fine, twenty-five," said Bob, frowning with impatience.

"Done," said Sam, holding out his hand.

Bob took it, his grip firm. Sam let go first. Bob picked up the wire fencing and carried it to Sam's truck. He offered to help but Bob just grunted, moving quickly and dropping it into the back of the pickup.

"Anything else?"

Sam shook his head.

"Things okay on the farm?" Bob asked the question while

staring over Sam's shoulder, like he was trying to make it sound casual but didn't quite know how.

"Yeah," said Sam. "Had a cow with a twisted stomach this spring though. You know how birthing always causes problems."

Bob chuckled through his teeth. "Ya lose her?"

"Nope. Had to put her on her back though. Roll her around a bit. Had a helluva time. Boys I hire don't quite have the muscle for it."

"Can't imagine going to so much trouble for a cow," said Bob, staring at him as if it were a challenge.

Silence for a moment.

Hick like you ain't gonna be nothing if you stay here.

"I'll bring the milk over later. You around today?"

Bob nodded as Sam opened the door of the cab and got inside.

"Say," said Bob through the cab's open window. "You seen my boy lately? Miles?"

Sam sat still for a moment, key in the ignition. Bob was looking at him now.

"No," said Sam. "You want me to keep an eye out?"

Bob's lips curled again. "Hard to keep track of them sometimes," he said. "Not that I guess you'd know."

Sam clenched his teeth and nodded goodbye, turning the key and gunning the motor. Bob rapped his knuckles lightly on the hood of the truck before turning and walking to the trailer. Sam put the truck in gear and rolled down the driveway, the Doberman's black eyes following him, cold and sharp in his rear-view mirror.

JOSH

W here have you guys been? I've been looking all over."
He leaned his bike against the side of Matthew's
house.

"I've been following Andy around for ages looking for the
compass," said Matthew. "He lost it somewhere."

The clouds had disappeared and the boys squinted in the
bright light.

"North," said Andy, touching the handlebars of Josh's bike.

"Miles Ford has it," said Josh quickly, as if he had to get the
words out before he could take another breath. "I saw him with
it a couple of hours ago."

"Where?" asked Matthew.

"By the river."

His bike fell over and Andy jumped back clutching his
hands to his chest. Josh shook his head and picked up the bike.

"We gotta get it back," said Matthew. "He must've stolen it
from Andy."

"Maybe he just found it wherever Andy left it."

But Matthew wasn't listening, his face dark, teeth
clenched.

Josh climbed onto his bike. "Let's just go ask him."

"Leave your bike. I wanna go slow. We gotta find him."

As they walked down the driveway, Josh looked back over his shoulder and saw Andy following at a distance.

"He stole it from him," said Matthew again, as they headed for the stop sign.

AVRIL

She poured Beth a glass of water and took it out into the backyard. The woman stood looking at the small vegetable garden. For the first time Avril thought about how old Beth seemed, how grey and frail. Beth thanked her and pointed to the string that ran from pole to pole above the chicken wire fence enclosing the vegetable patch.

"What's this for?"

"It keeps the deer out," said Avril. "They see the string and think they have to jump over it. Although Bob Ford told me he just uses pigs' blood."

Beth made a face. "I find it hard to believe there's a garden anywhere near that place."

Avril laughed softly. A breeze rolled through the backyard and the deer strings swayed on their poles, drooping like telephone wires.

"How's Al?"

Beth sighed. "He's . . . well, he's painting again."

"That's good, isn't it?"

Beth shook her head slowly, and at first Avril wasn't sure whether she was saying no or just thinking.

"Maybe. He told me he thinks Carson's still alive. He . . . he dreamt it."

Avril held her tongue, waiting to see if the woman was finished. Beth sipped her water, her eyes still on the garden.

"And you?" Avril asked finally, putting her hand on Beth's shoulder.

Beth smiled weakly at her and Avril could see she was holding back tears.

"It's been four days . . ."

They stood in silence until a dog nosed Avril's leg and she jumped. "Oh, I didn't see you there," she said, bending down to pat the dog's brown and black head. One of the mutt's ears drooped.

"Is he yours?" asked Beth.

"No, but we feed him sometimes. Seems like he's always hungry."

Beth clicked her tongue and frowned.

"What's wrong?"

"Well, it's just that Al feeds him too. He comes and goes though."

They both looked down at the dog, its tongue hanging sideways out of its jaw, its dark watery eyes staring at them as if waiting for the punchline.

AL HENRY

He sat studying the face on the canvas. He'd used char-coals, although he couldn't quite decide why. There was something about the image that wouldn't translate into colour. He'd seen the boy often enough, but he couldn't remember his name for some reason. A bit of an outcast, that one. Like his father.

The image had come to him early that morning, and now that it was out, he began to think about it. It wasn't nearly as accurate as painting from a photo, but it still resembled the boy well enough. And it was the second neighbour he'd felt compelled to draw or paint. Did it mean something? Strange somehow to see a face in shades of grey. What was the boy's name?

His mind moved quickly from thought to thought, unsettled. The vision of his son's plane was still so vivid he'd been tempted to check Deloume for signs of the crash. For years he'd thought his mother was crazy, all her talk of ancestors, spirit guides and visions. But something had found him, starting with the face of Joseph Choi. And then the vision, or dream, call it what you will. Or was it just wishful thinking? Thing was, he'd spoken to the bush company again that morning and they'd mentioned a co-pilot. And his son almost always flew solo. What were the odds?

Al had flown with him once, right over Deloume Road and Mount Baldy. Deloume such a strange strip cutting through the wilderness, and Mount Baldy with its skullcap, the arbutus tiny from the cockpit window. The Otter could carry a few passengers too, but there wouldn't have been any people on a cargo flight. Other than the co-pilot . . .

He tried to imagine what his mother would have said about his dream. She probably would have told him a story, something about Raven rescuing Sun from Seagull, or the one about Raccoon teaching Raven how to fish—tried to show him that there was more to life than met the eye. Guilt in the pit of his stomach. He would have listened now, if she were alive.

A dog barked and he looked out the window into the late morning light.

He went outside in his slippers, the sun's heat catching him off guard. A slow breeze rolled through the leaves of an arbutus, and a flying ant carried a tiny twig past his head. The long grass at the sides of the short driveway was sun-bleached yellow, almost white, and the three-foot blades leaned.

The porch light above him was still on and he reached back inside and flicked it off. A dead moth lay at his feet. No doubt it had burnt itself to death on the bare bulb. His stomach tightened. Again a feeling that something had found him. Joseph Choi and Korea. Carson and the crow.

Mul juseo.

God's country.

He grabbed a sketchbook and a few pencils from his studio, then returned to the porch. He drew standing up, first the arbutus that marked his driveway, its knotted trunk and arthritic branches, its oval leaves with their white centre strip. No colour now though, just shapes and shading. Then the bark, its cracks and lines, the way it peeled.

It was an arbutus on a mountaintop that our people tied their canoe to during the great flood. It kept us anchored.

He paused and held the sketchbook at arm's length. Then pencilled in a background, Mount Baldy, and Eagle above in the blocky Coast Salish style. It should have been a woodcarving, but paper would have to do. And there it was, the past he'd chosen to ignore.

A memory. This one of his son's airplane. On the side of it, where in his military days there might have been a voluptuous woman, was a painting of Eagle in black, white and red, with Coast Salish words in black below: *The Guide.* He'd laughed then, told his son that his grandmother would have been proud, and his son had responded without smiling, telling him that she was. That had been two years after her death. He never should have laughed.

God, just let the phone ring. Please let it ring. And then he felt dread in his gut. What if the call came and his vision had been wrong?

He looked down at the hasty sketch, trying to focus on his art, stay calm, force himself not to hold his breath.

The sun was hot now and sweat ran over his bare feet and into his slippers. He returned to his studio and tore the picture from the pad, tacking it to the wall so he could see it better. There was something about the smooth shapes of Eagle that agreed with him. Maybe the geometric unity of the animal reminded him of the contours of an airplane, of polished metal through cloud. Above the tree and mountain it seemed to work, belonging and not belonging all at once.

The paintings of airplanes on the wall looked so finished, so overly precise, and his eye caught the charcoal face of the boy still resting on his easel. He reached out and rubbed some of the charcoal shading around the boy's eyes that seemed too sharp, darkening the circle beneath each eye slightly. Then the name came to him.

SAM TOEWS

He leaned on the fence, the wire digging into his palms. On the other side stood the butcher. The man's forehead creased and stayed wrinkled. He seemed to be squinting at him.

"Look," said Sam, "I know you're just worried about the kid. That's fine. But here's the thing: he ain't yours."

The butcher nodded. Squeals from the roofed trough erupted then stopped abruptly. The farm baked in the heat around them.

"I know," said the butcher. "But I want to help. Don't you?"

"Well now, I have a strict policy of minding my own business." Sam spoke slowly. The butcher's accent had thickened throughout the conversation, and it was getting more and more difficult to understand.

"But a child is our business, I think," said the butcher.

Sam stared at him. The man didn't know what he was messing with. The Fords weren't going to let some foreigner tell them how to raise their kid. The butcher was right though. And that was the sad thing. He was arguing the wrong side and it made him feel short of breath, exasperated.

"Look, I know how you feel." He straightened up and let his hands drop to his sides, trying to look like he meant what he was saying. "But you can't mess with other people's ways of doing things. Especially not Bob Ford's. He'll be pissed if he thinks you're interfering."

Not to mention beat the living hell out of you, he thought, as the butcher nodded again, looking him in the eyes and mumbling thanks before turning away. Sam watched him walk back towards the pig troughs. It wasn't that he didn't want to help the Ford kid out, but Jesus, if anything happened to Miles on either of their farms there'd be hell to pay, no matter the whys or hows.

His neck burned in the heat and he turned the collar of his shirt up as he walked home, watching the midget shadow at his feet mimic his steps.

July, 1899

He cleared and weeded the area around the Douglas fir again, giving the fragile apple saplings room to breathe before he left for Bald Mountain. For the end. Moses didn't make it to the Promised Land and neither would he. His time was past. Fire from the sky lit the bush. The rope chosen and heavy.

Mapmaker screamed overhead and a murder of Scavengers took flight from the giant lightning-struck tree, flapping past him, their shadows fleeting through the unpolished-pearl dawn.

He was out of money and his men were furious.

I'll get paid or it's your life, Deloume.

But they would come to see what he'd given them. See the promised land as their inheritance. The land titles theirs forever.

What in hell's this, then? Land titles? To where? Here?

A mule deer stepped out of the trees and froze, staring at him, its ears twitching.

"Your name is Shy," he said, as the deer bounded away. "And we have that in common."

He clutched his compass as he waded off his path towards the mountain, a thick rope in his canvas sack, the promised land given away to men with wives and children. The chosen people. Families who would learn the broken hallelujahs of bent sword ferns, the meditation of root through earth, communion of huckleberry to lips and river-water baptism.

Mad as a mountain lion.

There's nothing here. Trees and trees.

Could clear it though. Be good farmland.

He breathed the mossy air. Mosquitoes whined in his ears and a hummingbird hovered beside him, drinking from a phoenix-orange honeysuckle. It was two days' walk to the summit through towering ferns and salal, and one question still nagged at him.

"So," he said, raising his voice to the treetops, "who will tell me my name?"

And each leaf and root and insect, each bird and animal called it out, and he heard it as wind through maple leaves, rushing through his ears.

Your name is Beginning.

THE BUTCHER

He stood outside the small shed, trying to focus on the black telephone wires along Deloume. They fuzzed and blurred. He tried to push Sam's words back, forget them. The man was kind, but he was wrong. Miles needed his help. He held his hand up to his face and waited for his eyes to focus on the lifeline of his palm. Then he looked across the pig farm at the trees around the pig graveyard, trying to bring them into focus. Shades of green and brown, gentle movement in the slow wind.

He suspected that Miles wouldn't be able to sleep in the shed much longer anyway. It would be cold soon. Something would have to give. Miles was a smart boy, he could sense it, but Sam's warning played through his mind again. Maybe the boy would hurt himself, or get sick. Maybe the boy's parents would blame him, point their fingers at the foreigner, come storming into the deli and demand to know what he'd done to their son, even if they did beat him. He was immediately ashamed. Just because he was foreign didn't mean he was allowed to be self-ish. If he was going to worry about Miles, it had to be for the boy's sake. He knew what he'd do to protect Petr. But would anyone here believe him? A foreigner?

His mind was skittish, moving fast, and he tried to catch his thoughts like flies. He argued with himself about when to pick up his glasses. Would Maria think he looked like an old man when she saw him wearing them? He hoped he'd hear something from her soon.

Home. It'd made so much sense to leave but he still missed it. Even though the promises of liberation from Russia seemed far-fetched. Always soon. Never now. Soon there will be books in Ukrainian again. Soon your children will have good high schools. Soon Chernobyl will seem like a bad dream, fading to less than nothing.

The explosions had only happened a few years ago but nothing about them felt like a dream. He'd had friends in towns near the accident who'd been outside enjoying the warm spring air. So mild for that time of year, they'd said. Sixteen weddings that day in their towns alone. And now the men who'd rushed in to clean up the Russians' mess were getting sick and staying that way. No help from the state, of course. People were still dying. His cousin was dying, his veins full of poison. He'd been a liquidator. What a title. They'd told him to go and build a wall around Chernobyl. Told him not to worry, that it was safe. So why build a wall?

So what was it exactly that he missed? Perhaps just family. He wondered if he'd still miss the place once Maria and Petr arrived. Perhaps that was all home was. Family. A family he wished so badly he had now. Perhaps that was why he couldn't stop thinking about Miles. The boy didn't have a family either. Not really.

He stood staring at the sky, watching small clouds as if they were billowing smoke, poison, fallout. As if they had followed him across the ocean. Contagious death.

The midday sun beat down on his head and a line of sweat trailed from his temple down his cheek. Not as hot as a few weeks ago though. The weather seemed to be changing for the better. Albeit slowly. Cool afternoons would help him work.

He stepped into the deli just as a woman entered, and he squinted at the outline of her brown curling hair spreading out like watercolours over wet paper, her mouth a blur of rusty lipstick. She moved closer and came into focus, smiling and asking for sausages. He wrapped the meat for her.

She thanked him and left. It was getting bad. How long would it be before he wouldn't even recognize his own wife if she came through the door? If it stayed relatively quiet he'd close the shop early and pick up his glasses. Forty years old, and already his eyes were bad.

He squinted through the open front door at the mailbox outside. Maybe the postman had forgotten to turn up the red flag. A letter could have arrived. Or more than one. A stack of letters delayed somehow. It happened all the time back home. People in his neighbourhood were always receiving mail from relatives asking for a place to stay weeks after they'd come and gone, or love notes after love had disappeared, or letters from the dead.

He took fast steps to the mailbox and opened it decisively. A quick look. Even without perfect vision he could see it was empty.

Another customer, a man this time, buying pepperoni. Said he was from Mill Bay. That was a good sign. People must be talking about the deli. Making detours on their way home from work. The butcher didn't bother to weigh the meat, relying on touch to know that he'd thrown in extra. The man thanked him twice and said he'd be back. It was a good day for business, so why couldn't he just be content? A letter would come. They would come. Visas, passports, a mess of red tape. It all took time.

He leaned his elbows on the counter. Just another hour or so and then he'd go. He rubbed his eyes. They were getting tired and watering.

Footsteps on the tile floor.

"Just a moment," he said, wiping his eyes on his shirt sleeve.

The tear-blurred outline of a boy.

"Petr?" he said, before he could catch himself.

The child didn't speak. Instead the boy held out his hand and dropped something metallic on the counter. He wiped his eyes again. It was Miles.

"I'm sorry," he said. "My son's name is Petr, and for a moment you looked . . ." He let his voice trail off.

Miles coughed and then spoke quickly, as if he'd rehearsed the lines. "It's a present. It's for you."

The butcher had assumed the metal click on the countertop was a coin, but he saw now that it was a metal locket.

"It opens," said Miles.

The butcher opened it. A compass.

"Well," he said. "It's wonderful."

He hesitated. The silence grew awkward, Sam's warning a constant whisper in the back of his mind. He needed time to think, but the boy was waiting for him to say something. Waiting for him to take the gift, staring at him without blinking.

"Please," he said to the boy. "You keep it."

Miles tilted his head and coughed again, as if unsure of how to deal with a change in the script. The butcher closed the metal locket and stretched over the counter, holding the compass by, what was it, a shoelace? The compass dangled, a pendulum between them.

"I c-c-can't," said Miles.

"Please," said the butcher. "You should have it. It's a wonderful thing, and a wonderful gift, but I can't accept it. I want you to keep it."

"I can't," said Miles again, but the boy's expression didn't change as he took the compass and left the deli.

Had he done the right thing? Of course he had. How could he accept a gift from a child?

MILES FORD

He walked at first but then broke into a run, no destination in mind, just away. The butcher had hated it, probably hated him too. What had he been thinking, trying to give a grown-up a present? A compass. What would a butcher need a compass for? He wasn't lost.

Miles reached the river and climbed down to his hiding spot. A brown bat took flight from its upside-down roost, and he ducked as it shot out of the pipe. Smells of root, steel and earth mingled, and he held his breath to hear the faint trickle of water, barely audible, barely moving over stones.

He cried quietly, sniffing and taking short, shaky breaths that echoed off the round metal. He couldn't face the butcher again. He would have to go back to the trailer, back to the junkyard. All at once he wished he were the butcher's son. He imagined living in the small cottage on the pig farm. Everything would be different. He'd be surrounded by animals instead of junk, and there would be someone who noticed when he came and went.

"And what would you like for your birthday this year?" the butcher would ask.

"A new bike," said Miles, his voice bouncing off and around the pipe. "Red."

And Matthew and Josh would be jealous of the bike, would

see it and ask if they could have a turn. At first he'd refuse, but then, once they'd followed him around for a while, he'd let them ride it. Like friends.

He wished he hadn't thought it almost immediately, and he wiped his nose on his sleeve as the images faded. They hated him too. They'd rather play with Andy. With a retard.

Why hadn't the butcher taken the gift? He tried to tell himself again that it was because it was stupid, a piece of junk that the butcher didn't like, but somehow, alone with his thoughts beneath the road, the idea didn't quite fit. The butcher was a nice man, not like his father, and he gave him food, a place to sleep . . .

Maybe the gift was too good. But he'd found it. Someone had just thrown it away. He took the compass out of his pocket and let the metal warm in his closed palm.

Just enough light crept through the root-covered ends of the pipe for him to see the oval outline of his gift. He had wanted so badly for the man to take it with wide-eyed amazement.

"I've always wanted one just like this," said the butcher.

And he'd find more gifts to bring, steal them from the junk-yard outside his parents' trailer if he had to. There were all sorts of things hiding there, under tires and inside old refrigerators. Tools and sometimes keys.

"Amazing," said the butcher. "I've never seen anything so perfect. I know just what I'll do with these."

But the butcher hadn't taken the compass. Hadn't wanted it.

"Why bring this garbage into my shop?"

"It's a present," said Miles, his voice pleading and cracking in the dim pipe.

"Get out," said the butcher. "Go home where you belong."

No. He hadn't said that. He just couldn't accept the gift. There must be some rule Miles didn't know about. He had to try again, to make the empty feeling in his stomach go away, to make the butcher take it.

He wiped his eyes on his shirt and put the compass around his neck. He climbed out of the pipe and down to the river to wash his face. He bent down and cupped water, splashing himself, his blurred reflection rippling in the pool.

Another face appeared above his own, and he felt his heart slam into his rib cage. The face was underwater, no, behind him. He whirled around and scrambled to his feet.

"Give it to me," said Matthew, his face expressionless.

The boy's fists were balled.

"What?" asked Miles.

"It's mine," said Matthew.

Miles followed the boy's eyes to the compass hanging from the shoelace around his neck. He clenched the metal locket and stepped back.

"I-I found it," he said, his heart racing.

"Where?"

Miles pointed at the river.

"You stole it from my brother." Matthew's voice was loud now. "Give it back."

"It's a present, it's not yours," said Miles, surprised that his own voice came out so forcefully.

Matthew looked startled but seemed to recover, stepping forward again, close enough to touch.

"This is your last chance," said Matthew.

Miles looked down at the compass in his hand. "But I . . . it's a present."

Matthew lunged forward and grabbed the compass, pulling him down by the shoelace around his neck. Miles flailed his arms and grabbed one of Matthew's wrists, and then the shoelace with his other hand, pulling back.

He couldn't believe the speed of it, how everything around him blurred, the pain of the shoelace biting into his neck, the lace too thick to snap. He let go of the boy's wrist and lashed out, his fingernails digging deep into Matthew's arm. The boy pulled away, blood and peeled skin in three lines down the inside of his forearm.

Both boys stood panting.

Out of the corner of his eye Miles caught a movement in the shadow of a tree beside him, and as he turned to look, Matthew yelled and swung his fist, hitting him in the middle of his chest. The air left Miles's lungs and he stumbled backwards to the edge of the river, clutching his chest, the compass still swinging from the shoelace around his rope-burned neck.

Again Matthew leapt forward, tackling him into the water, the shock of the cold and the pain in his chest leaving him panicked for breath, and he shoved Matthew's flailing body off him and struggled to find his footing.

The water was only a few feet deep and he stood up gasping, blowing out spittle and water and snot.

He wiped his eyes and saw Matthew coughing beside him, doubled over, the boy's face a few inches above the water. Miles felt for the compass but the shoelace had fallen off. The water was brown and clouded, mud and leaves swirling up from beneath his feet.

It was gone.

His breath was back now, fast but ragged, and anger welled up inside him as the shock of the blow and the cold began to wear off, and pain from the rope burn on his neck and the bruise on his chest spread. He took one step and then leapt on Matthew's back, forcing him under the water, letting his weight push the boy down into the clouds of silt.

MATTHEW

The scratches on his arm burned, and lines of blood ran down to his wrist and hand. He'd never been in a fight like this before, and as pain spread over his arm one thought seared through his mind: *He stole it.*

Miles stood within reach and Matthew hit him as hard as he could, feeling his knuckles connect and pop as they slammed into the other boy's chest, and still the compass swung from Miles's neck.

Stolen from my brother.

He lunged forward, tackling Miles at the waist, cannoning the two of them into the cold river. He lost his bearings as soon as his head hit the water and he grabbed at Miles beside him. Miles kicked him away and the force of the blow caused him to suck in water.

Weight in his lungs and a mad scramble to find his footing. His shoes struck bottom and he pushed himself up violently, surprised when he emerged from water only waist high. He doubled over coughing, the muddy water pouring from his lungs and still no air. Finally a wheeze of breath and more coughing, lungs tight, eyes open now, staring at the brown water. And then Miles was on top of him, the boy's full weight pushing him underwater, fingernails digging into the back of his neck, his hair gripped tight, shooting pain through his scalp and head. He flailed his arms, trying to turn, his feet slipping on the bottom and out behind him, nothing to hold, nothing to grab, his hands sinking in mud as he tried to push up. And still the weight of the boy on his back, hands pushing his head under. He fought the urge to inhale, his chest on fire.

He tried again to turn but this time his muscles failed him and he stopped moving, found himself counting to ten. And then he'd breathe in.

... seven, eight, nine ...

JOSH

G et off him!"
But Miles didn't flinch, face ashen, jaw tight, and his hands on Matthew's head and neck, his friend's blood mixing with the water. He yelled again, watching Matthew's arms flail.

Drowning him.

He ran to the edge of the pool. His toe dislodged a stone, twice the size of his hand but oval and flat, white and grey.

Now.

He picked up the rock and jumped feet first into the water, his shoes heavy with each step. Again he yelled, grabbing Miles's shoulder, pushing him. The boy's muscles were tight, his hands still on Matthew's head, his friend not even struggling now, maybe dead.

Josh swung his arm as hard as he could, heaving the rock sideways, the stone connecting with the back of Miles's head with an odd thud, like a fist into dough on a kitchen counter, then slipping out of his hand with the impact and into the water. Miles's arms dropped to his sides and the boy toppled forward, face down.

MATTHEW

The weight lifted and he raised his head just above the water and gasped, blood pounding in his ears.

He knelt on the bottom, too tired to do anything but breathe, the cold-stone taste of water heavy in his mouth.

Ten. Ten. Ten.

The number rolled through his mind with his pulse. Hands grabbed his arms and he went limp, no energy to fight, fuzzy black dots blurring his vision. Short, rough breaths.

Ten. Ten. Ten.

But he wasn't forced under again, instead he was dragged to the edge, his head rolling back. Movement of leaves, cracks of sunlight, then up onto the bank, where hands pushed him onto his side and a wave of nausea hit. He vomited water and lunch and then just retched, dry-heaving as the cold started to spread. Black fuzz and a haze of images, Miles clutching the compass, swirling dark water.

He retched again and his body contorted in a spasm of racking coughs. Finally the haze lifted and he opened his eyes wide, felt the sharpness of pain from the scratches on his arm and scalp. He propped himself up on his elbows and waited for the dizziness to pass. He breathed deep and let it out slowly. Then again.

Josh sat next to him, soaked from the waist down, staring at him, his eyes bugged out and his face sheet white.

"Are you . . .?" said Josh, stopping and taking a shaky breath.

"Yeah," said Matthew, his throat burning from the stomach acid. "Miles?"

Nothing.

Matthew closed his eyes again and sat up, felt a tree behind him and leaned back, shifting his legs and backside among the roots, the pain on his scalp intense, coming and going in rhythm. He touched the back of his head and neck and looked at his hand. Blood mixed with twigs and dirt in black clumps.

Josh's shoulders and chest were heaving, his mouth spread wide and open thin, his eyes scrunched.

"It's okay," said Matthew. "I'm okay."

Josh shook his head.

Matthew felt his muscles relax and he stopped shivering as the summer air warmed him. But now his friend began to sob and shake and gasp in short bursts.

"Where's Miles?"

He tried to stand but found he couldn't yet, and he slumped back against the tree, dizzy. He focused on Josh until his vision cleared. His friend was staring at the river. He shuffled around so he could see what he was looking at.

Miles floated face down, deep red spreading out through the water from his head, not in a cloud but in stringy lines, like carmine roots making their way through the copper water, clearer now as the silt settled, patches of sunlight illuminating the sinking blood. The body floated limp, turning ever so slowly in the slight current of pool and breeze, leaving behind an arc of blood, and for a split second he felt nothing, a hurricane-eye stillness, then just the heaviness of his eyelids.

JOSH

A *teaspoon of water.*
   Someone had told him that was all it took to drown, flood the lungs, die.

He looked over his shoulder at the pool. So much blood, as if a paintbrush had been dipped in a glass of water for cleaning, and it spread from Miles's head in veinlike threads, more and more of it, the boy's waterlogged shoes heavy and sinking, his arms and hair just below the surface. Blood so dark.

He took a step forward, willing his feet back into the water, but his legs went numb and he crumpled onto his backside, hugging his knees, unable to look away from the pool.

Matthew breathed in high-pitched whines. His friend lifted his head and said something that ended with "*Miles,*" but the words didn't make sense, became a jumble of sounds mixed with his own sobs and the great rushing of air around him, and he stared at the boy in the river, just stared.

Silence. Then each noise alone: heart on rib cage, breath to lung, throat stuck to sob, Matthew's voice, loud now, awake.

"We gotta get him out."

Josh shook his head, closed his eyes.

"Help me! Come on!" said Matthew, grabbing his arm and pulling him.

Josh stood up, saw Matthew stride back into the river then become shaky, unsure of each step. He followed.

Together they grabbed Miles, an arm each, and pulled him to the edge of the pool. Neither of them spoke and he barely felt the cold water on his feet and legs.

So much blood.

They rolled him over in the water and both let go, stepping back in shock.

Miles's face was turning grey and white in patches, eyes staring up, mouth wide like a choirboy's.

Matthew recovered first, grabbing an arm, and he did the same, the two of them heaving the water-heavy body onto the bank. Blood continued to pour from the wound onto earth and dry leaves, pooling beneath the boy's head, his eyes so wide, so still, unblinking.

ANDY

Not asleep. Eyes open.

His brother and Josh pulled the limp body onto the edge of the riverbank.

He felt the tree's bark with both hands, the tiny bumps and pockets of sap, the heaviness of the tree as he leaned on it and peeked around to watch.

Miles's feet flopped out, limp sneakers, waterlogged and still.

Three boys.

He ducked behind the tree and counted to himself in a whisper.

"Matthew one. Josh two. Miles three . . ."

He leaned slowly around the tree to see them. His brother argued with Josh. Lips moving. Josh crying.

His brother's voice. "We have to hide him."

Hide.

His mind raced through kitchen cupboards and under beds, to tree forts and tents, behind the woodpile, behind a tree.

One Mississippi, two . . .

Tones now, sound and light from above him, rays of sun onto his hands and the tree trunk. So warm. He pushed his fingernail into a sap bubble on the bark and the golden liquid oozed onto his finger. He breathed the sharp bitterness of it and touched his finger to his thumb, the sap sticking as he pulled them apart.

Tree glue.

More words in the air, Matthew and Josh raising their voices.

"I can't!" said Josh.

"You have to!" Matthew's voice high, cracking. "We'll bury him deep. I think the butcher's gone for the day. There's a sign on the deli door."

He stared at Miles until his eyes watered and he blinked.

Bury.

In his sandbox digging until he reached a layer of cool wet sand, dropping a green plastic soldier inside.

Green. One. Bury.

And then the avalanche of dry sand into the hole, covering the tiny soldier.

He tried to wipe the sap off his fingers but they just stuck to his shirt, now finger, thumb and shirt were all sticky, then pants.

Matthew leaving. Up the riverbank into trees towards the pig farm. Josh stood over Miles, quiet now, looking down at Miles's face. Josh took a step back, his lips moving, bits and pieces of sound. "No. No . . ."

"No," whispered Andy.

Matthew back through the trees with a shovel and hoe, the wooden handles taller than him.

"We can't," said Josh. "It's wrong."

"Do you want someone to see him?"

Josh shook his head. "But where?"

"On the pig farm. The graves. My dad told me they're for sick pigs that die and you can't eat."

He could see blood on his brother's neck and arm.

Be careful.

Matthew dropped the shovel and hoe and picked up one of Miles's arms.

"It's cold," he said, grimacing.

Josh picked up the other arm and together they dragged Miles away from the river through the trees towards the pig farm. Grey shoes trailing, digging lines behind them.

When they were out of sight he moved away from the tree and walked to where the river was shallow enough to cross. Josh crashed back through the underbrush. Andy froze, Josh looking straight at him but not saying anything. He stood motionless, holding his breath, waiting.

Josh raised a finger to his lips.

Andy let out the breath and touched his own lips.

"Shhh."

Bitter sap and he gagged as Josh picked up the tools and disappeared back into the trees. He spat until only a dull aftertaste remained, then followed the boys across the river.

He crouched in the bushes on the edge of the farm. Green around him. Hiding him. No voices. Thud and chink of hoe on loose stones and earth. The smooth sound of the shovel. Bone and black earth. A crow cawed from a tree branch and he shivered, felt the sound move through him, the hair on his neck prickling.

Then Miles into the hole.

Bury.

Josh's lips moving. Asking Matthew.

His brother's voice answering. "I only know one prayer. We used to sing it at school when we were little. It's about Johnny Appleseed."

Josh silent. Staring at the hole.

"I can't really sing good," said Matthew.

Bitter sap. He let spittle drop from his mouth to the ground in a string, afraid that if he spat his brother would hear him and send him away.

Talking again. "Your brother was by the river," said Josh.

Andy tensed up.

Brother.

But Matthew just shook his head. "He doesn't know what he sees."

Then Matthew's voice. Wavering. Thin sounds.

> *"Oh the Lord is good to me,*
> *and so I thank the Lord,*
> *for giving me the things I need,*
> *the sun and the rain and the apple seed,*
> *the Lord is good to me.*
> *Johnny Appleseed, Amen."*

Silence. Then another shuffle and flap of a crow's wings and its caw, and the metal-to-dirt noises of the shovel and hoe filling in the hole.

"One Mississippi, two . . ." he counted quietly.

Sweet leaf smell. Manure.

Josh speaking. "Do you think the butcher'll find him?"

Matthew shook his head. "I think this is an old one. That grave over there is fresh." He pointed to another mound of brown dirt.

Andy held his breath again, like when his brother let him pretend to hunt with him. Fern spears. He watched his brother take the tools back across the farm. When Matthew came back the two boys gathered leaves and grass and spread it over the fresh dirt, then disappeared back into the forest.

Andy took a long, noisy breath once they were gone. "Bury," he said, picturing the plastic soldier lying still and deep in the sandbox.

Migration

The Canada geese fly over in Vs, cackling and honking.

I stand on the road and look for you through heat waves. The sun prickles the back of my neck. A cobalt butterfly wafts on the berry-flower breeze. Grey rock spiders and beetles crawl along the road's edge, and tiger-striped caterpillars cling to alder branches above. I turn over a stone with my toe, scattering pill bugs and a centipede.

I see you out of the corner of my eye, a shadow flitting behind trees.

I walk back past gravel driveways with car-tire tracks up their edges and spaces along their middles where grass grows. A dog's bark carries on ahead of me down the road towards the stop sign.

A boy sits beneath the wires along Deloume, his blond hair bleached by the summer sun, his eyes shocking blue, his nose freckled and his lips August dry. He's lying on his stomach propped up on his elbows watching a line of ants, tiny titans carrying worlds of twigs and seeds on their backs. The boy watches the ants' inch-by-inch pilgrimage towards an underground nest. The ants have been busy all summer, preparing for the first crystal frost, but the boy watches them as if he's never seen anything quite like them before.

I stand beside him as he fades into heat waves, colours, then disappears.

Gravel and tar have hardened along the edge of the road, and pieces hang from thousands of small fault lines. I pick up a chunk that has slid into the ditch: a tiny continent. I throw the piece of road into the air and when it hits the ground it breaks into countless pieces, leaving a black stain at the point of impact.

Across the road and up a driveway, a half-finished painting sits on an easel outside, the paint drying in the sun. The subject is an arbutus, its roots clinging to a rocky patch of earth. The red bark of the tree peels in strips, curling off the trunk like aging paper. Beneath the peeling, rust-coloured bark lies pale almond flesh, with hints of green around the bare strips.

A woman waddles down the road. Her swollen breasts pull the top of her pale blue sundress taut at the shoulder straps, and her belly button causes the fabric to bump. The blue cotton cascades down to her smooth brown ankles. Her black hair is pulled back and her high cheekbones frame her face, her dark eyes watching a snail mark the ground, its shell a swirl of amber and maroon.

I smile but she walks past me, her dress blurring at the edges, becoming part of the scenery, the air, then gone.

I keep walking, faster now, past the stop sign to the pig farm, where a man in an apron sits outside listening to pigs push each other into the boards of their feeding stalls. The squeals seem to come from animals breathing in instead of out. At the end of the farm maples and cedars hide the pig graveyard. The cedars' gown-like boughs drape to the ground and crows by the dozen look clumsy on their branches, swaggering awkwardly, like children wearing Halloween costumes that don't fit.

I wave at the butcher but he doesn't move.

Footsteps beside me through the wheat grass along the ditch.

I find myself collecting sounds, trying to hold them in the glass case of my mind, trying desperately not to forget them, as if this will bring me peace. No metal-frame shudder of bikes through potholes. No war cries or murmur from the pipes below Deloume. The sounds of laughter replaced by silence.

Your body turning in water, skull cracked.

I turn my back on the farm and pick up a rock, warming the stone in my pocket as I retrace my steps to the stop sign, sizing it up from across the road. The distance seems so much smaller than it used to. My stone hits the sign with the solitary clang of a church bell.

I climb down to the river and stare into the water, the sun playing its usual flashlight tag through leaves with the surface. I blink and look at the inside of my arm, at the fingernail marks, the lines of scar tissue pink and uneven, still vivid after all this time.

Another V of Canadas above, this one lower and louder. Even the crows look up.

AL HENRY

He sat on his front porch as the breeze bent grass and shuffled leaves like a deck of cards. A new sheet, white and crisp, sat before him on the easel. He practised on paper now, not ready yet for canvas. He pencilled it all in first, working out the details of the traditional art, allowing himself to make mistake after mistake. The porch was less claustrophobic than his studio, especially now that the temperature had fallen a few degrees. Aw, who the hell was he trying to kid? He couldn't work in the studio because he'd just end up staring at the phone, wondering what the temperature was doing farther north, willing the damn thing to ring.

His hand shook slightly and he botched a curve. He straightened his back and his spine cracked, his muscles tense and sore from sitting. Through the kitchen window he could hear Beth opening and closing drawers as she prepared lunch. Keeping busy. Waiting, just like him.

Footsteps shuffled up the driveway. It was Irene. He put down his pencil, surprised to see her out and about.

"Hi." She smiled at him and blushed.

Her hair was tied back and her eyes seemed bigger than they had before, wider, as though she too were surprised by her visit.

"Out for a walk?" he asked.

She nodded and smiled again, her hand moving up gracefully to cover her mouth. A pale blue sundress fell from her thin shoulders over the half moon of her belly. She fidgeted with her fingers.

"Are you here to see Beth?"

"No, I . . ." She hesitated, searching for words in the air above him. "I came to ask about your son," she finished.

"Oh," he said. "Carson's . . . well, there's still no word . . ."

"I'm sorry."

They stared at each other.

"I see you are busy," she added, turning to leave.

"No, no," he said. "Just taking a break."

A pause.

"Thank you for the painting, Al," she said quickly, and he smiled at the rehearsed line. She struggled with the *l* in his name, and it came out sounding like something between an *l* and an *r*.

"You're welcome. Has Beth ever told you what my real name is?"

Irene's brow wrinkled. "Not Al?"

"No. I go by Al because it's easier. Just like Irene, right? That's not your real name, is it?"

She shook her head. "What is your real name?"

He told her. "Hard to say, isn't it?"

Irene tried to repeat it but only managed the first syllable. They both laughed. It was nice to see her smile, to hear her laugh naturally. The sound had been missing from Deloume somehow, as though he'd been waiting to hear it but never realized.

"What does your real name mean?" she asked.

"Well, it means . . . actually it doesn't really have a meaning in English. It means what it is. Sorry, do you have any idea what I'm talking about?"

"I understand," she said. "English doesn't always work."

"Yeah. So, I told you my secret. Now it's your turn. What's your Korean name? Will I be able to pronounce it?"

"Sue Hwa," she said, then bit her bottom lip, waiting for him to respond.

"Sue Hwa? That's not so difficult."

"No, but I wanted an English name, and Joseph . . ." Her smile faded.

"I see," he said quietly.

His chest tightened. She felt it every day. At least he still had hope.

"So, does your name mean anything in English?" he asked.

"Water flower," she said, her voice soft but her pronunciation clearer. She knew those words well.

"Lily?"

"No." She shook her head. "Different flower. Hydra . . ." she mumbled. "Ah. Hydrangea."

He smiled.

"I will keep walking," she said, bobbing her head forward in a half bow and then catching herself.

"You're welcome to stay for lunch if you'd like. I'm sure Beth would like to see you."

"No thank you," she said, running her hand over the hair above her ear, checking that it was still pulled back in place. "I will keep walking," she repeated, her posture so upright, belly so heavy.

He nodded and said goodbye, watching her slow walk back down the driveway past Beth's garden, where blue flowers hung from their bushes in round clumps.

The phone rang inside and he stood, bumping into his easel and sending it rocking. His heart pounded and he was afraid to move. The ringing stopped as Beth answered it then came to the door, her lips moving without a sound, eyes wide. She grabbed his arm and pulled him into his studio. He adjusted to the dim light of the room slowly, sunspots flashing as he blinked and Beth pressed the receiver into his hand.

"Hello?" he said.

A burst of static and the crackle of a poor connection.

"Can you hear me?" came a voice through the interference. "It's me."

IRENE

It had been a long time since anyone had called her by her Korean name face to face. But it hadn't been hard for Al to pronounce. Not like his name had been for her. Maybe she would ask Beth to call her Sue Hwa too.

Her feet ached and her back was tense and sore in places. But the sun on her head and shoulders was the perfect temperature, hot but soft, the sharpness passing south, leaving behind only an inkling of summer in the air. And the road was so quiet, no cars, but it was busy in its way too, with all the insects and birds.

At the end of Avril's driveway sat a boy, blond hair and tanned arms. She could tell by the way he watched the ground that it was Andy. She'd seen him in that exact spot before, watching and counting. Last time it had been tent caterpillars. She walked towards him and looked at the ground. A line of ants this time. She wanted to tell him to thank his mother again for the lasagna, but she wasn't sure if he'd understand.

"Hi," she said, surprising herself again.

Andy looked up at her stomach and smiled, his front teeth large, with bumps along the bottom, proof of how new they were. He had freckles, just a smattering over his nose, and his eyebrows were sun-bleached almost white.

"Counting," said Andy.

"How many ants?" she asked, speaking slowly. It was always easier to talk to children.

"Red, black," he said.

His eyes hadn't left her round belly. She put her hand on it, smoothing her sundress.

"Baby," she said, and then felt a wave of panic.

Still no movement. No kicks. She'd asked Beth to call her doctor and set up an appointment for tomorrow, and she tried to push it out of her mind again. Stay calm.

Andy put his hand on his own stomach and leaned back, pushing it out. "Baby," he said. "Two."

She shook her head. "No, only one."

"One," said Andy, exhaling and letting his stomach and back relax.

She tried again, pointing at the line of ants. "How many?"

Andy looked down at the line, his eyes following its curving trail into the undergrowth.

"Red, black. Two."

They watched the ants together, their relentless march from hidden to hidden, the unbroken line. She felt the urge to speak. To say all the thoughts that she'd been holding in her mind, as if collecting them, precious and unusable.

"My husband is dead," she said in Korean.

Andy's eyes didn't move from the line of ants. Again she spoke in Korean.

"He's never coming back."

What was she thinking? Andy couldn't understand. She switched to English and said the words slowly.

"He is gone forever."

The words didn't come out broken or sad though. They just hung there. She stood silently, feeling the August air on her shoulders and arms, her body heavy, like it was supposed to be.

"Gone," said Andy. "Bury."

"Yes. He is," she said. Then, "I live here."

This time Andy looked up. "Live," he said, staring over her head.

His eyes were clear and blue. They seemed light, unburdened. He stood up beside her and looked down at the ants, and she watched his face, a smile spreading as if he'd just seen the insects for the first time. If she told Andy her secrets he would hear them but not remember, carry them like letters, her words less than the weight of paper.

"I'm going to stay here," she told him.

"Two," he said, still looking at the ants.

"Even if my baby isn't alive."

The words skipped off her tongue like stones over water, there and there and there and gone.

There was no life waiting for her in Korea, only old memories and friends who wouldn't understand how she'd changed. Just thinking about Busan and her family and everything people would say about her made her tired. But here, anything could happen. Al and Beth would help her. Maybe she'd get a job eventually, work in Mill Bay or Victoria. Even if she was carrying death. Even if it had spread to her like a sickness.

Please . . .

Andy stepped back from the ants and faced her. The boy took long, deep breaths, as if he had to be conscious of them to make them happen. He stared at her belly and she tried to stay still, afraid to move in case she broke the spell. In the corners of her eyes grass rippled in the breeze, branches swayed, leaves rustled. A dandelion top rolled along the tarred gravel, collecting dust and dropping its spores until it was just a stem. A yellow bird fluttered from twig to twig, its wings bright against a backdrop of leaves. She blinked and watched Andy stare at her.

He stretched out his hand slowly, fingers up, palm towards her.

"Baby," he said.

It felt so long ago now, that afternoon when he'd touched her stomach and run away, Avril rolling her eyes and laughing with her.

She smiled and the edges of her mouth cracked. She took Andy's hand in both of hers, felt the heat of his skin, the small softness of his fingers, and pulled his hand gently forward until his palm rested on her swollen womb.

The baby kicked hard, like it had been saving its strength, and she winced, still pressing Andy's hand against her. Then again, tiny foot to rib, and only when she saw how wide Andy's eyes were, felt his fingers tremble, did she realize what it meant. She let go of his hand and laughed when he didn't let it drop, instead holding it up and staring at it like he had the time before. She felt tears start and then she had to pee, and she turned and walked quickly, looking back over her shoulder at Andy, who was still watching his hand.

And as she walked, a thought came to her and she held on to it, repeating it over and over with each step.

I'm going home.

THE BUTCHER

He readjusted his glasses, the skin on the bridge of his nose stinging. The raw skin didn't matter though, the optometrist had assured him it would pass and that soon he would forget he was even wearing glasses. Part of him hoped not. The miracle of sharp lines was so shocking that when he'd first put them on he'd just sat in the doctor's office staring at the eye charts with his mouth open.

He looked around the deli now in amazement. The crisp geometry of the countertop to the floor. And the wooden door frame. His vision had been deteriorating for a while but he hadn't realized how slowly, and he wasn't sure if he'd ever seen the place properly.

He was embarrassed that he'd called Miles Petr. It was a mistake he wouldn't make again, not now that he could see clearly. What a fool he'd been, acting like a stubborn old man, refusing to pick up his prescription.

Had he made the right decision to give back Miles's gift? Surely it was the only thing of value the boy owned. At least, he'd never seen the boy with anything else. He was still bothered by the strange look that Miles had given him. It had been so blank, a shuttering of expression. What had it meant? Maybe he could explain himself to the boy, tell him how grateful he really was but that he already had so much, and Miles had so little . . . No, that wouldn't do.

He was worried that Miles had gone home. And to what? Another beating? He stepped out the back of the deli and looked across the pig farm. The telephone wires were clear lines. There was no blurring. His forehead relaxed. The branches of the trees were clear too, textured, soft and alive in the afternoon light.

He imagined Miles and Petr playing together, throwing stones at the stop sign and learning how to feed the pigs. And they could go to school together, and maybe, if he could afford it one day, they would have bicycles.

He could see now that he had no excuses. He lived on Deloume. It was his home, and he wouldn't just pretend he wasn't a part of what happened here. Not any more. He couldn't make his own family arrive quicker, but he could confront the Fords. And maybe there were others who would go with him, maybe that painter and his wife, or the Korean woman. They had been kind any time they'd bought meat from him. And the parents of other children on Deloume, of Matthew and Andy and Josh. Surely they would understand, feel the same way he did. Sam had warned him about interfering. But maybe Sam was just afraid too.

He looked across the pig farm again to a gathering of crows in the trees at the far end. So many for such a warm afternoon. Surely they should have been resting in the shade like everything else that time of day. Strange. How long since he'd buried a pig? Several days. It was something else then. As he looked at the trees, at the colours and lines, he realized that what the doctor had said had come true. He'd already forgotten he was wearing glasses.

He kept looking at the crows. He really should go and see what all the fuss was about. He could go to the Fords' later. Or was he hesitating because he was scared of the confrontation?

He walked across the dry ground. It was his job to check. His duty. Perhaps it was an injured animal. He stopped when he reached the graves. One of the mounds had been turned over, the dirt dark. He hesitated and then scolded himself for being silly. Someone had probably run over a neighbourhood dog and been too ashamed to find its owner. Those dogs were always chasing cars. It had only been a matter of time. He'd have to track down its owner. That was what neighbours did. The right thing.

He fetched a shovel and dug quickly, turning over the soft earth easily. Above him the crows squawked and wrestled for position along branches. He blocked out the sound. Finally his shovel hit something soft. He levered it up, expecting the hind leg of a dog, then dropped the shovel and stepped back. On the surface of the dirt, exposed and pale, lay a small, earth-stained hand.

JOSH

He sat alone beneath the Doug-fir. The skin under his eyes stung from crying.

A conversation with Matthew a million years ago in the same spot.

"Do you believe in heaven?" he'd asked.

And Matthew had nodded. "I hope I go there when I die."

"Yeah, me too."

Something stiff pricked his neck. A large, dark brown eagle's feather jutted from a fold of rough bark.

He pulled it out and ran his finger along the smooth dark ripple.

Magic. If he really believed, it would make him fly.

The sound of dirt falling onto a body, the small thudding of tiny stones and earth on chest and shoulder and leg. The scraping of a shovel blade through the ground.

He gripped the feather tight, crushing it and sobbing.

"I didn't mean it," he said, his voice throaty and cracked.

MATTHEW

He ran to the washroom and threw up in the toilet. The image again: white face, eyes open.

He wiped his mouth on his sleeve, his head spinning. He sat down on the small yellow floor mat, leaning against the porcelain bowl.

The fingernail marks on his arm were swollen. Skin puffed out on both sides of each tear. He guessed it was the same on his head and neck.

He threw up again, dry-heaving over the toilet, his whole body retching, muscle spasms in his gut, his throat on fire. He took tiny breaths until his eyes focused on the toilet seat. He ran his hand through the sweat and blood in his tangled hair.

Someone banged on the door.

"Matthew?" It was his grandpa. "That you in there?"

"Yeah," he croaked.

"You sick? Come unlock the door."

Matthew stood up, his legs shaky. He opened the door and his grandfather caught him as he stumbled forward.

"What the hell happened to you? Shit, you're bleeding."

He had to lie. He had to think of something. He could blame his brother, say that Andy had flipped out, started scratching him. Or that he and Josh had got into a fight. But his thoughts tumbled into each other and dizziness spun him into a daze.

"The pig farm," he said, appalled as the words left his mouth.

"What? Where's Andy? Who did this to you?"

JONAH DAVIES

He held the boy's hand as they walked down the road to the near end of the pig farm and along the fence separating it from the small river. He carried a shovel in his free hand.

"This damn well better be important. Half a mind to take you straight to a doctor."

The bleeding had stopped, but the scratches on Matthew's neck and arm looked bad. Must've been one hell of a fight. He wondered what the other boy looked like. It better not've been Andy.

"You gonna tell me why I'm lugging this shovel around any time soon?"

Matthew shook his head. "It wasn't supposed to happen."

"Damn it boy, you're scaring me a little."

He needed a smoke but he tried to forget about it until he figured out what the hell was going on. He had a weakness for the kid, no doubt about that. Who else would he go on some wild goose chase for?

Matthew stopped and pointed to a mound of dirt. His hand shaking.

"This one of those car-chasing dogs?"

He drove the shovel into the ground, digging quickly through the loose soil until he was turning out white pig bones. After a few minutes he stopped and looked at Matthew.

"We here to dig up dead pigs?"

Matthew looked at the hole then at the other grassy mounds. The boy looked confused, shocked even.

"This deep enough for you?" He sighed. "Damn it all, you've got a fever, don't ya? I knew I should have taken you to the doctor. Your mother'll have my hide for this."

He grabbed the boy's hand, pulling him back towards the road, but Matthew jerked away, trying to speak, his voice rasping, his eyes never leaving the hole. Finally the boy mumbled something he couldn't make out.

"You got something to say?"

Matthew's lips moved as squeals and shuffling echoed across the farm, the pigs fighting frantically for space at the feeding trough, their high-pitched whines drowning out the boy's voice.

THE BUTCHER

He staggered back from the pen as the pigs squealed and jostled, pressing closer together. He closed his eyes as the noise grew louder.

For Petr. And Maria. Forgive me Father.

SAM TOEWS

He stood out on his driveway watching an old man and one of the neighbourhood boys, Matthew, he thought, emerge from the back of the pig farm with a shovel. He walked to intercept them, shouting until they stopped. Matthew was in rough shape, blood drying in his hair and on one of his arms. The man wore a cowboy hat and boots. Sure as heck wasn't local.

"You two all right?" He looked at Matthew, trying to hide his shock at seeing the boy looking bad.

"Who's asking?" said the man.

"Sam Toews. My farm," he said, jerking his head back towards it.

"Jonah Davies. Avril's dad. My grandson here's gotten into it with somebody, but I'll be damned if he'll tell me anything."

"What's over there?" asked Sam, nodding at the pig graveyard.

The man looked at his grandson, but Matthew was staring at the road, lips tight.

"Beats the hell outta me. He's got me digging up dead pigs."

The hair on Sam's neck stood on end and his skin crawled. He looked at the old man and then at the boy again. It was Matthew's eyes. His breathing. Not right. Shocked. He'd seen it with cows before, that wild panic.

"Look, let me give you two a ride home."

The old man seemed to think about it but waved him off. "It ain't far, thanks."

He started to protest but the old man just shook his head and led Matthew up Deloume by the hand towards Avril's place. Sam walked through the ditch to the back of the farm between the fence and the river, to the pig graveyard. They'd turned over a mound of soil. Bad thoughts flapped through his mind like bats, blind but sure all the same, dark and moving fast. Then he noticed the trail of turned-up earth and he followed it down to the river, found the leaves on the bank dark with blood. And lots of it. Coulda been Matthew's, but he reckoned it was too much— the kid hadn't looked that bad. Whose then? Just the sight of it was making him sick. Cow's blood was one thing, but this . . .

He headed back out onto the road and made for home, hearing the truck approaching him from behind but afraid to turn around, his stomach churning, twisting.

"Out walking?" Bob pulled up beside him and leaned out the truck's window.

Sam nodded. "Just met Avril's dad. Nice fella. We got to talking." He spoke quickly, the words intentional and forced. He didn't know nothing for sure. Had to be careful.

Bob grunted. "Had a kid with him, did he?"

Sam nodded again. "Matthew. I seen you out driving a couple times today. Something wrong?"

Bob hesitated and ground his teeth, his jaw working side to side. "Looking for my boy. Farmer like you musta been outside nearly all day."

"Sure. On and off."

"And?"

Hick like you ain't gonna be nothing if you stay here.

Sam stared straight at the man's beady eyes. "And I ain't seen nothing Bob."

Bob sniffed and spat out his window as Sam turned and headed for home, the slow rumble of the black truck growling at his heels.

AVRIL

She walked down Deloume holding an ice cream pail in one hand. The sun cast telephone-wire shadows at her feet. She scanned the sides of the road, stopping at the largest blackberry bush she could find. They were late this year, but there wasn't any harm in trying. She stepped over the ditch carefully, scanning the bush for ripe berries. She pulled one off and tested it. Still a little sour. Some of them had spots of red. Maybe she'd have to wait another week. Or she could just take a few of the darkest ones for a batch of muffins. The sourness wouldn't matter much then. She'd have to bring some around to the neighbours if they turned out all right. Irene was due in a matter of days. She pulled off another berry and dropped it into the bucket.

When she'd collected enough she headed home, taking her time in the sun, letting her mind wander. Matthew was looking better, his cuts healing fine, angry as they'd looked. Why he and Josh would ever get into it with one another was beyond her. It had never happened before, but boys were boys. And really, no broken bones was good news, even if the scratches had been deep. She'd spoken to Josh's mother and she'd been just as mystified. Neither of the boys wanted to talk about it and Andy had been as cryptic as ever. So what was there to do?

It frightened her how shaken up Matthew had been, but maybe that was just because he and Josh were such good friends. It wouldn't be long before they'd be riding up and down the road together again, steering with one hand and chewing on pepperoni sticks from the butcher.

The whole thing seemed to have upset her dad more than it had her. She was probably just jaded from seeing so many cut knees and bloody noses over the years. He'd left a couple of days after it'd happened. Not suddenly exactly, but she could tell seeing Matthew like that had bothered him. Maybe he wasn't such a tough cowboy after all.

The road seemed to stretch out before her like a dried-up riverbed. It was one of those days that made summer feel permanent, a season that would go on forever. All of the other seasons were times to look forwards or backwards from. But not summer. Summer was a time to *be*. She tilted the bucket as she walked and heard the berries roll.

She paused by the Fords' driveway. There'd been talk about Miles lately. That he'd run away, that Bob was out looking for him. Just as likely social services had intervened though. God only knew what went on in that trailer. She felt a twinge of guilt at the thought. What was it about Miles that made him so easy to forget? He had a way of just sliding in and out of her mind like a bird's shadow over Deloume.

She saw that Bob had nailed a plywood sign to a telephone pole, the words in black paint: *Lawn mower for sale. Like new. $60.*

ANDY

He watched his brother lean over the river, stretching his arms and using a cedar branch to try to hook the shoe-lace that floated up from the compass on the muddy bottom.

"North," he said, but his brother didn't respond.

Miles floating.

Not asleep.

Matthew wobbled on the edge of the river and struggled to regain his balance, waving his free arm in half-circles. White bandages covered one of his arms and the back of his neck.

"Careful. Be careful," said Andy, and this time his brother looked at him. He dropped his eyes and stared at the water.

Miles's face. Red spilling from his head.

Be careful. North.

Water gliders dimpled the surface and he leaned towards the river, watching the bugs' tiny feet resting on the water's skin.

He blinked and his eyes refocused on his own reflection. Dark face. White eyes. Finally Matthew hooked the shoelace with the branch and pulled the round metal locket off the bottom. He dropped the stick and held the compass by the shoe-lace, staring at it without blinking.

"North," said Andy, holding out his hands.

Matthew shook his head. "No, not this time."

"No," repeated Andy, kneeling and leaning over the water again, nose close to watch the gliders.

"Don't fall in," came his brother's voice.

Be careful.

Miles moving slowly, turning in the water. And then his brother's voice again.

"Andy? Are you listening? Be careful."

He nodded and reached towards the water, the tips of his fingers hovering above the pool's surface.

August, 1899

They found him hanging from an arbutus. Crows at him.
Eyeless.

Lord, he said something about the mountain here, but I . . .

Told you he'd gone mad Ford. Who ever heard of payin' in land titles?

Swinging there, neck bent, skin scorched and dry. Wind-
burnt. And trees stretching out as far as sight below.

Anything in his bag?

A compass. Some drawings and maps. Not much.

Can I take the compass? Always wanted one.

Like hell Toews, it's mine.

MATTHEW

"You should have it," he said. "You saved me."

Josh turned away but not fast enough to hide the tears. "I don't want it."

They stood hidden among alders and salal just off the side of the road. The late afternoon air was cooling fast and Matthew stuffed his hands into his blue nylon windbreaker. He only had a couple of bandages left on his arm and the healing cuts and scratches itched like crazy.

"They're never gonna find him. He's gone."

"You keep saying that! But where? How?" Josh's voice was shrill. He wiped his eyes. "I don't want it anyway."

Matthew felt his stomach go hollow as he turned and left Josh in the woods and walked home alone, the compass cold in his pocket.

The Compass

I walk down Deloume Road, dragonflies baking fluorescent in
the sun and telephone lines whispering prayers from pole to
pole ahead of me.

Maybe you watch.

A mangy brown and black dog trots alongside me, snapping
absently at a yellow butterfly that rides autumn's breath over
the dog's one flopping ear. The butterfly lands on an abandoned
berry-stained ice cream pail, shutting its wings overhead and
casting a thin, sundial shadow.

I pause beside the stop sign and hold out the silver locket,
let it slip from my palm then close my fingers on the shoelace
attached to its clasp. I hang the locket from the sign, hooking
the shoelace over a jagged bit of metal in the rusted gap where
the O should be.

The compass swings for a moment, dangling from the sign,
then is still.

ACKNOWLEDGMENTS

Thanks to:

Shawna Grace for the encouragement and close readings.

Ben Wright for the countless hours of reading and editing.

Richard Francis at Bath Spa University for the calm advice and patience.

Also at Bath Spa University: Richard Kerridge and Trischa Wastvedt, as well as Joseph White, Jane Forrest, Sabrina Brody, Victoria Owens and Dann Casswell.

David and Sayuri in Bath and Göran and Annika in Stockholm for the hospitality while I was writing this.

Louise Dennys at Knopf and Alex Bowler at Jonathan Cape for the excellent editorial advice.

And finally, my agent Will Francis in London, without whom this manuscript would be just another notebook among notebooks or worse.